MW01093748

DRAGONS OF
DESERT AND DUST

What readers say about Susan Brown's "Dragon Books"!

DRAGONS OF DESERT AND DUST:

Fourteen-year-old Angel is on a desert treasure hunt, searching for valuable turquoise stones with enough power to break through the dusty chokehold on his life. Will the visions that appear and the dragon talisman he wears be enough for him to soar as the eagle does, to freedom and a noble destiny? – Torri McEntire

"An absorbing mystery set in the desert Southwest that conjures the mystical experiences of Angel, as he confronts the meaning and relationships of his splintered life." – Virginia Alonzo

An intense story with graceful pacing that puts you in the shoes of Angel Cerillos as he longs for adventure and freedom in the New Mexico Desert. I simply could not stop reading!" – James Henry

"*Dragons of Desert and Dust* pulls you in. You can taste the dry dusty air and your own heart thumps wildly as you're taken on Angel's adventure in the desert of New Mexico." – Heather Wong

DRAGONS OF FROST AND FIRE

"Imaginative, new and incredibly captivating from the very beginning. From the first words, I was invested in Kit's story." – McCulloch L.

"*Dragons of Frost and Fire* is an engaging read that leads the reader into a mysterious and wild world. Trying to find the clues in Silver Claw with the lead character keeps you at the edge of your seat, and all through the book bright descriptions of the Alaskan wilderness are creating a stunning setting in your mind. What a fantastic read!" – Seven Bennett

"*Dragons of Frost and Fire* is a wondrous tale full of mystery, and of course dragons. This is a book you won't want to put down!" – Rayen P.

DRAGONS OF
DESERT AND DUST

SUSAN BROWN

YELLOW FARMHOUSE PUBLICATIONS
LAKE STEVENS, WASHINGTON 2016

Copyright © 2015 Susan Brown

All rights reserved. Except for use in any review, the reproduction or utilization of this work in whole or in part in any form by any electronic, mechanical or other means, now known or hereafter invented, including xerography, photocopying and recording, or in any information storage or retrieval system is forbidden without the written permission of the author. This is a work of fiction. Names, characters, places and incidents are either the product of the author's imagination or are used fictitiously, and any resemblance to actual persons, living or dead, business establishments, events or locales is entirely coincidental.

ISBN-13: 978-1514162194
ISBN-10: 1514162199

Susan Brown's website: www.susanbrownwrites.com

Cover design: Heather McIntyre, mcintyre.heather1@gmail.com
Cover photos: Dragon Eye by anekoho; Cave by specularphoto

Interior design:
Heather McIntyre, mcintyre.heather1@gmail.com
And Roland Trenary

Times New Roman
Herculanum

Acknowledgements and Special Thanks

Go out to the students at Henry M. Jackson High School who inspire me with their enthusiasm and dreams,

To the Writers Cooperative of the Pacific Northwest whose members advised, edited, and supported me in bringing this book to completion,

My writing partner Anne Stephenson (aka 1/2 of Stephanie Browning) who keeps me inspired to work on this and our joint writing projects,

And especially to my three daughters, Laurel, Heather, and Karen, who put up with me through the creation of this book (and many other things) as well as reading and encouraging every day.

Thank you!

DRAGONS OF
DESERT AND DUST

ONE

Facing east toward the mountains, Angel Cerillos dug his toes into the loose slats of the shed's roof. As the sun shimmered across the New Mexico desert, he lifted his arms upward, feeling the turquoise talisman warming against his chest like a piece of desert sky.

"The eagles are my brothers..." he chanted. He swept his arms downward in the eagles' curving wing thrusts, imitating how they soared over the parched mountains.

"I am greater than the eagles..."

Eyes drifting shut, his mind flew skyward.

"I am king of the skies...." The rhythmic beat, beat of his arms echoed the chant. He could hear the singing clearly now – there, just beyond the horizon. A thrumming chant that was getting louder and louder, day by day. Magic singing that no one else heard....

"Angel! *Angel!*" Treese Tanner's voice cracked through the dream. Arms still flapping, his feet skidded on the tin roof. Scrabbling with fingers and scraping with toes, he slid along the burning metal, and then down over the edge.

A cry tore from his throat. He flew now, but straight down, slamming onto the hard-packed dirt. Gasping for breath, he saw his foster mother loom like a black shadow against the sky. Treese Tanner's lips pursed and she jammed her big hands on her hips. The hot wind blew her badly-cut hair around her head like a faded halo.

"Y'okay?" she asked.

Angel tried to answer, but all that came out was a raspy grunt.

"Can you get up?" she demanded.

He wheezed again, and thrashed like a bug on a pin. She stared back, exasperation evident on her weathered face. "You deserve to have broke every bone you got," she told him. "Fourteen years old and you don't have the sense you were born with. And those sad blue eyes of yours don't fool me. I seen the way you look at Gary when he pushes you too far. But you watch yourself around him – he can get mean."

"I know," Angel grunted. "I ain't gonna get in his way."

Treese snorted. "I don't think you'd hardly know anything, the way you're always mooning around."

"I can look after myself." Angel stared up at the sky, wishing he could fly up there and away from his life.

"You need someone to watch out for you, kid, but I'm not the mothering kind, so you be careful. Now, get up. Put your shirt on. We got work to do." She turned and headed toward the front of the motel. Angel stayed where he was, lying in the dust, waiting for his breathing to get back to normal.

For a moment he had thought his secret chant was going to work, thought that the haunting dreams and whispering voices would be satisfied and stop. His only friend around here, Celsa Reyna, had helped him come up with words that sounded like an old Indian chant. He had even come out here early – not sunrise exactly – but as close as he could manage without an alarm clock. Spitting out a mouthful of dust, Angel sat up and stared into the gleaming blue sky. For a minute he had felt like he could flap his arms and rise into the air just like one of the eagles that soared over the motel. Felt like he could escape.

"*Angel!*" Treese called from the front of the motel. "Get a move on!"

"Coming!" Angel yelled back, even though he stayed put, looking up at the sky, drinking in the beautiful blue. For once he felt peaceful, not all torn up by the storms of emotion that rolled over him like thunderclouds on the mountains. Up until the state moved him here to the Lone Butte Motel he had been able to pull back, not get caught up in the fights and bad stuff around him. But there was something about this clean dry air, endless horizon, and blue sky that had him stirred up. Of course, life at the motel didn't help.

Treese sounded gruff, but she was all right. Angel mostly liked her. But his foster father, Gary, was a whole different deal. He could make anyone laugh with his jokes. His voice was silky and smooth. Everyone liked Gary. Everyone but Angel...and maybe Treese too, though she never said.

With a sigh, Angel got to his feet. He shook back his straight brown hair, tried to dust off his skin, then gave up and pulled on the loose shirt that was one of Gary's hand-me-downs. His foster father would be back from town soon with another case of beer. If the motel's rooms weren't clean and the beds changed, he'd be mad. That would mean the silky voice would get hard and if he'd already started on the beer, maybe he'd stop joking and start slapping.

For a moment Angel gripped the turquoise talisman – the only thing that he had left from his own family. His fingers traced the two-headed, horned snake, more like a dragon, with its long sinewy body looped back and forth and a fanged head on each end. Angel had had it as long as he could remember, strung on string or an old shoelace around his neck. "You keep that safe," his ma had told him. "It's your birth gift from your father."

And he did keep it safe. It never left him, no matter what. He'd figured there was some invisible magic on it because no one ever said anything about it and no matter how chaotic his foster homes were, the other kids never grabbed for it. They just looked and then their eyes slid away like they forgot they saw it. And mostly Angel forgot too. But a few months ago, around his fourteenth birthday, there had been a change. Sometimes, the carving seemed to hum like the high voltage wires that swayed high above the highway. When Angel held the dragon in his two hands, he'd felt a jolt of power. Everything he saw, heard, smelled and tasted seemed brighter, cleaner...more beautiful. His head swam and he felt himself soaring into ideas and visions that were new and frightening. And then...nothing. They just faded away. He didn't know whether to be terrified or thrilled. But those feelings had compelled him to try the Indian chant thing. Dumb.

"*Angel!*" The sharpened note in Treese's voice meant she'd spotted Gary's truck on the horizon.

"*Coming!*" Angel shoved the talisman under his shirt and sprinted towards the motel. He rounded the building's cracked adobe wall and grabbed the laundry cart he'd left by number18. By the time Gary's truck spun gravel into a cloud out on the parking lot, Angel was head first into the room's shower stall, scrubbing. The bed was stripped and the soiled laundry in the cart. Crisp, clean sheets that Treese had ironed last night were on the bed, and the faded bedspread had been smoothed over them.

Angel felt rather than saw Gary's presence in the doorway. He scrubbed harder, not looking up, knowing that even a glance might invite some kind of punishment if Gary was in a punishing mood.

"Well, can't you say hi?" Gary demanded.

Angel sat back on his heels and wiped his arm across his brow, hoping it would impress his foster father with how hard he was working. The man was big, a football player in his high school glory days, but now most of the muscle had slid down to his gut.

"Hi, Gary. I was scrubbing so I didn't hear you come in." Angel eyed the bottle of beer in the man's hand and kept his face carefully blank.

His foster father grunted. Before he turned to go, he shoved his big knee into Angel's shoulder blades, sending the boy sprawling head first into the shower stall. The cleaner streaked across Angel's cheek, burning. Scrambling back out onto the cracked tile, he used his shirt sleeve to wipe the soap from his face.

"Watch you don't slip there, boy." Gary snickered and sauntered out. "And move your butt," he called back. "If you want any lunch, all these rooms better be clean."

Angel slowly wiped his face again. His skin stung, and the earlier spurt of anger fanned into fury. He wished, he wished with everything he had, that Gary would be on the receiving end – just once. His hand crept to the turquoise dragon. The talisman burned in his hand, hotter and hotter. Angel shut his eyes and wished and wished.

A white convertible streaks toward the motel...a writhing shape skitters up from the dust devils that whirl across the road...the car swerves...spins into the Lone Butte parking lot...gravel shoots everywhere like dusty bullets...and Gary walks out of number 18, beer bottle tilted up. He doesn't see the spinning car...

The driver wrenches the wheel. The fender just side-swipes Gary, sending him sprawling in the dirt. The bottle flies from his hand, shattering on the stones, shooting shards of glass in all directions...

Treese's cry shocked Angel from the dream. He dropped the talisman back under his shirt and tore outside to see what was going on. Gary was sprawled in the dust, his hand clapped to his cheek. A trickle of blood oozed between his fingers. Broken glass glinted in the gravel and beer steamed away in the desert heat.

A big man in a suit and cowboy hat rushed from the sports car toward Gary. Treese came pelting from number seven. Angel pressed back against the motel wall, breathing hard.

"You all right?" the man asked, squatting by Gary.

"You crazy fool," Gary sputtered. "You coulda killed me." He wiped his arm across his cheek, leaving a streak of blood on his sleeve.

"I really am sorry," the man said. "I thought I saw an animal on the road, so I cranked the wheel and my car spun right out of control. That's never happened with this car before. I don't understand it. But are you all right? Should I take you into the hospital in Santa Fe?"

Gary struggled to his feet. The stranger rose beside him, offering a steadying hand.

Gary shrugged it away. "No, I don't need no doctors. I'm okay." He eyed the man and his pale eyes sharpened. "Say, aren't you John Hydemann? You own the Turquoise Hill Ranch, right?"

Angel sucked in his breath. The Turquoise Hill Ranch bounded the back of the motel. And kept on going to cover hundreds of square miles more – one of the biggest ranches in the state. Celsa and several other kids at school lived in the adobe cottages Hydemann had built for his hired hands. She called him King Hydemann because everyone jumped to do what he said.

"That's right. I'm John Hydemann." The rancher held out his hand.

Gary grinned, wiped his palm on his jeans, and stuck out his own hand. "And I'm Gary Tanner. Don't know why we haven't met before, being neighbors. I own and operate this here Lone Butte Motel." He motioned grandly. "It ain't much at the moment, but we're fixing it up. I plan to turn it into a resort and conference center – I'm thinkin' of an Anasazi kinda pueblo theme. But I'm looking for the right business partners. Men with vision. Like me and you..."

"Can I offer you some iced tea, Mr. Hydemann?" Treese interrupted. Angel could see the embarrassed flush on his foster mother's face.

Gary stiffened, but he kept the smile going.

"No, I thank you though." Mr. Hydemann nodded to her. "I have an appointment that I'm already late for. And if you're sure you're not hurt, Mr. Tanner..." He offered his hand in a farewell shake.

"Gary, call me Gary!" He shook hands. "I think I'm just fine. Been a pleasure to meet you, John." He leaned on the back fender of the gleaming white car like a good-natured pal.

As Hydemann turned to get into the car, he spotted Angel standing in the shadows. To Angel's amazement, the rancher smiled and included him in his wave. Angel didn't move but felt a brief surge of pleasure at being noticed.

That pleasure dulled his wits. He stayed when he should have slipped away, because as soon as the car became a white blur on the straight road, the friendly mask dropped from Gary's heavy face.

"Iced tea?" he demanded. "Treese, you stupid cow! A man like John Hydemann don't waste his time on iced tea..."

Angel knew where this was going. Gary would yell for a while, and then unless he got distracted he'd start whaling on Treese. Or Angel.

It gave him a sour feeling in his stomach, but there wasn't anything he could do. He hesitated for only a moment and then with the skill of long practice, Angel slipped sideways through the shadows and around the corner of the building. He broke into a run and cleared the sagging fence in a fear-sharpened leap

The desert spread out before him, reddish gold in the sun, mottled with tufts of grey and green shrubs. He kept on running, loping like a coyote. Behind him, in the distance, he heard Treese cry out once, making him break stride and stumble. Crouching, he clenched his fists and looked back. No sign of Gary. Just the same he sprang up and ran faster. His sharp breathing began to match the pounding of his feet. Dust rose behind him...and then he was alone and free.

TWO

The desert peace settled Angel's nerves, blurring away his flaming emotions. He slowed to a steady, distance-covering trot.

Out of long habit, Angel kept a sharp lookout for the men who worked Hydemann's land. Once he saw a vehicle's moving dust cloud, so he dropped to a crouch and stayed motionless, watching. But the cloud rolled away toward the foothills where the cattle grazed. When he judged the truck was too far away for the men to spot him, Angel rose to his feet again and loped across the landscape.

After a mile or so more, Angel reached a big, featureless rock that reared above the dust and juniper scrub. A smaller slab leaned against it, and a jumble of rocks lying over that had created a small cool cave, just big enough to hide him and his meager cache of survival gear: eleven discarded water bottles that he'd refilled, beef jerky in a screw top jar, and two worn blankets that Gary thought had been stolen by guests. Angel had smuggled it all out here over the three months that he'd lived with Treese and Gary. He'd long since learned it was smart to have a back-up plan.

He squatted for a moment in the hot sun to catch his breath, and then unbuttoned his shirt. The sun on the talisman shone like a piece of the sky – like he, Angel Cerillos, owned the sky itself.

"I am greater than the eagles..." he whispered. The sun washed across him, warming the cold places in his heart. He sniffed the air. The scents kept getting stronger, linking themselves to colors and emotions – making his life brighter and richer. Maybe it was the desert, not just the talisman. He sniffed again – dry juniper, dust, animal musk. Was he beginning to see and smell like the desert animals? Angel rubbed his palms across the rough earth, lifted his head and breathed deeply, allowing the desert to fill his lungs and heart. He'd rather live among the desert animals than with most of the humans he knew.

Thirsty, he knelt by his cave and breathed the cool air trickling from the crevice. It carried the scent of a small lizard but he didn't mind that, or even the desert rats or small rodents. He sure didn't want to stick his fingers into the snout of a rattlesnake though.

Reaching in, Angel gently shook the whiptail lizard from its perch on a water bottle. He watched as it skittered out of the cave and ran into a tangle of dry brush. With a long sigh, Angel slid down to sit with his back to the rock, unscrewed the cap and took a long drink. When he'd had enough, he groped to the very back of his hideout for his great treasure. He pulled out a knotted bandana, dusty, faded and a little frayed. His mom had given it to him before she became too lost in her mind to keep their little family whole.

Inside the bundle lay six sky-blue turquoise stones, each veined with slender black lines like spider webs. Valuable. Worth more than four hundred dollars. More money than he had ever had.

Not enough.

Angel rubbed each big nugget with his thumb, loving the smooth beauty. It had taken all the time he could steal away from the motel to find these six perfectly colored stones. Stones the color of the desert sky, the color of his eyes, and the color of the dragon talisman knotted around his neck.

Sitting back, rolling the stones in his hand, he remembered how he'd found one nugget on the second day after he'd come to stay with Treese and Gary. He'd thought it was pretty, but had not known how valuable it was until he met Celsa Reyna on the school bus.

School had had only seven weeks left in the year when his social worker, Mrs. Preston, brought Angel to The Lone Butte Motel. After four years of moving through seven other foster homes, he was existing in a state of stone-faced panic – terrified that he'd have to move again; tired of the way that the kids at every new school sneered at him; sick with loneliness. That first day, Treese sleepily fed him toast and peanut butter, handed him his battered back pack, and told him to wait at the edge of the motel parking lot for the bus to pick him up.

He did as he was told, standing like a fence post, staring down the highway, shivering in his thin jacket from the cool, early morning air. At long last the yellow bus pulled up and opened the door.

"Morning," the driver said as Angel climbed woodenly up the steps.

Mouth too dry to speak, he nodded at her.

"You're first on," she told him. "You get your pick of seats."

The door swung shut and she pulled back onto the highway before he had even sat down. He chose a seat in the middle of the bus, sliding over to the window, clutching his backpack. After a ten minute rumbling race down the highway, the bus lurched to a stop by the Turquoise Hill Ranch, and a gaggle of children and teens crowded on. The bus seemed to explode with their shouts and laughter.

A couple of boys, bigger and obviously stronger than Angel stopped in the aisle and stared at him. "Hey, new kid!" one of the boys said. "Whatcha got in that backpack?"

"Luis, leave him alone!" A girl about Angel's own age bundled three young ones into seats opposite him and then took her time to look him over. Her eyes were chocolate brown and serious, set in a wide square face. Her long, dark hair was thick and curling, swept back from her face and fastened with embossed silver clips. Angel couldn't help but notice that she looked rounded, soft and full. Pretty in a way that made him feel warm.

When one of the teens poked her, she turned from her study of Angel.

"*Hoye*, Celsa, you gonna make me?" the bully was laughing now.

Celsa tossed her head, making her thick hair swing. "No, Luis, I'm going to get *chiquita* Miranda to do it. She's in first grade, so she's ready for someone like you!"

The boys laughed and when the driver roared at them, sauntered to seats at the back. As the bus lurched back onto the highway, Celsa slid into the seat beside Angel.

"*Hola,* I'm Celsa Reyna," she said, her voice as rich as fudge. "Just ignore these *javelinas.* They're only half awful but they'll bully you if you let them. They're learning from their *papás* and big brothers."

Not knowing what to say, Angel stared out the window.

"So what's your name?" She regarded him with interest. When he didn't answer, she went on. "*Mi mamá* heard at the food mart that you're living at the motel. I told her that makes no sense. Doesn't that cost a lot to stay there?"

Burning with hot shame, Angel glared out at the landscape. Celsa kept her eyes on his face, but said nothing else. She did not seem to be in the least offended that he did not speak to her. At last, the bus dropped the little ones at an elementary school, and then drove a block to the high school. All the other teens, including Celsa, got out, leaving Angel alone in his seat, clutching his backpack, hoping he didn't throw up from nerves. Then Celsa leaned back inside the door.

"The office is right across from the front entrance," she said and disappeared again.

Throwing his backpack over one shoulder, Angel left the bus and went into the echoing school.

He had long since learned to freeze his face into a mask of sullen unconcern, but every moment terrified him as he tried to find his classes and was repeatedly late. In the swirl of strangers, he twice saw Celsa and three times heard her voice and deep laugh. Even though he didn't call out to her or do anything to attract her attention, she was like a lifeline to something familiar. Luis and his friends were in his math class, but they ignored him. In the cafeteria Angel found out no one had done the paperwork for him to get free school lunches. He had no money and Treese hadn't given him any lunch, so he sat alone at a table and tried to pretend he wasn't hungry. When Celsa slid onto the bench beside him he forced out a "Hi again," and followed it up with what he hoped was a friendly smile.

She smiled in return and without speaking divided her own large lunch; she pushed a ham sandwich and a honey-drenched sopaipilla in front of him.

Angel ate the sandwich and savored the sweet pastry after it. "Thanks," he said at last.

"*Esta bien*," she told him. "You look like you could use a friend. But you still haven't told me your name."

"My name's Angel Cerillos, and I'm fine," he said.

She examined his expression, doubt obvious on her face. "So, where else have you lived? Anywhere interesting?"

Angel shook his head, pushing the crumbs into a neat pile, then onto the floor. "Albuquerque for awhile. Santa Fe for a few months. No place good."

A bell rang for the next class. Celsa rolled her eyes. "There's never enough time at lunch to have a conversation," she complained. "I want to hear about where you've lived. Anywhere has got to be more interesting than around here."

She rose and walked away, heading toward her classes. Angel consulted his rumpled schedule, and went in search of yet another classroom.

Later, when Celsa sat beside him on the bus, one of the boys hooted. Angel stared out the window, burning with embarrassment.

"Shut up, Georges!" Celsa called toward the offending kid, then smiled at Angel. When he didn't acknowledge her, she poked him. "Tell me about living in Santa Fe," she commanded.

Angel shrugged. "I was only six. My mom worked for a jewelry shop." He remembered the shop and the artists who came in to sell their work while he had sat in a corner, coloring, watching, keeping quiet.

"What kind of jewelry?"

"Silver mostly. Some turquoise like this." He dug the nugget from his pocket and showed it to her.

"Where'd you get that?" she asked.

"Found it a couple of days ago…in a ditch in the desert."

"Let me see." Celsa examined the nugget on her palm, poking it this way and that with her fingertip, a frown gathering on her face. "*Oye!* That's high grade. Worth good money – really good money. You'd better hide that or you'll be in more trouble than you ever want to see."

"Why?" Angel demanded. "I just found it lying around the desert."

"Don't be dumb. There are already too many stupid people around here," Celsa retorted. "All the good turquoise belongs to *señor* Hydemann because all the land belongs to him. Everywhere. Miles and miles of land. A few people, they mine little claims by hand – make stuff for the tourists – but there's only one place and one mine in New Mexico where you can find this color of turquoise. It's up there in the hills." She pointed out the dusty window toward a bluish purple rise on the horizon.

"But this was just lying there!" he protested. Angel's attention fastened on the most important thing Celsa had said – *worth a lot of money.*

"Doesn't matter. *Señor* Hydemann owns it," Celsa stated. "And he makes sure nobody gets it. The ranch hands ride around in trucks just looking for trespassers." She leaned forward and tapped the girl sitting in front of them on the head. "Tania, tell Angel about what your brothers did yesterday."

Tania turned around so that her deep brown eyes and bushy hair rose above the back of the seat. "They got two students from the university," Tania said. "Carlos and Ritchie chased them with the jeep, and then they tied them up and took them back to the house. Even though they were crying and all, *Señor* Hydemann called the state patrol. *Mi mamá* said he'll probably make them go to jail."

"Can he do that?" Angel wondered uneasily what the rancher would do if he discovered the foster kid from the motel had already started roaming the desert.

"He does it," Celsa replied. "You see those signs?" She gestured out the bus window. Every few yards, weathered tires hung from fence posts with KEEP OUT painted on them in big white letters. "See! That's all he had to do, and the law is on his side. All the men, even my own brothers, think it's a great sport – hunting trespassers." Celsa poked his arm. "Nobody goes anywhere on *señor* Hydemann's land unless he says they can – not even us and we've lived there for ages. King Hydemann's crazy – a crazy tyrant. What does he think hikers could hurt in the desert? Phooey." She made a noise like she was spitting on the school bus floor.

Angel laughed. She turned her fierce eyes on him. "It's no joke! Some of his men are real bullies, Angel. They'd push you around before they even took you to *señor* Hydemann."

Embarrassed by his reactions, by the warmth of Celsa's shoulder near his, Angel only nodded, but when the bus rumbled down a side road he caught sight of a yellow *Yield* sign shot full of holes. Maybe Celsa wasn't just trying to scare him.

But did he really care? The blue stone was worth money and more stones would be worth more money. If he found enough, he could help his mom. Leaning his forehead against the dusty window, Angel stared out at the desert, rolling the stone around and around in his hand. Off in the distance, the hills lay rumpled like an old quilt, tufted and drab. There was turquoise hidden in those folds of rock, and to get it he would risk Gary's anger and Hydemann's bullies.

Turquoise would save his mother and set him free. And that was all that mattered.

THREE

After his first conversation with Celsa, Angel thought constantly about turquoise. Treese had lived in the desert all her life, so a few days later, while they washed up the supper dishes, he asked her about the gemstones.

She shrugged. "Most of the old mines are up in the foothills... here, watch you don't chip my Tweetie Bird mug...the mines all belong to John Hydemann, of course." She reached for the pots and dunked them in the dishwater. "Everything around here, kid, belongs to Mr. Hydemann, except this motel. This bit of land has been in my family a long, long time."

Angel stacked the cups in the cupboard. "But can't people just find turquoise around?" he persisted.

"Oh, I don't know. A few folks prospect in the back country away from the big ranch, but they don't seem to find much. They say the old Indians, y'know them Anasazi that all just up and vanished...?"

Angel nodded. There'd been a unit at his last school about the ancient Pueblo Indians who had mysteriously disappeared nearly five hundred years ago.

"Well...I heard them Anasazi had turquoise mines so big and rich, there were whole secret caves of it. They mined turquoise for centuries – traded it to other tribes all up and down the countryside, even down into Mexico. But I guess those old mines are all used up or maybe just lost."

"But I...um...heard kids talking at school – about how one of them found a turquoise nugget out in a ditch." He glanced under his lashes at Treese.

"Yeah, I guess a person might find some – y'know, washed down by the floods in the arroyos."

"The what?"

"Arroyos – they're the dried up stream beds. Except after the rain in the mountains, they ain't dried up. I half drowned in an arroyo when I was a kid. We get these storms out here – like the whole sky is broken open. Lots of crashing thunder, and the rain comes down like someone's emptying barrels out of the sky. That water rolls on down the mountains into the arroyos – floods so quick you can hardly get out of the way. Whoosh!" She snapped her towel at Angel. He grinned.

"And what about the turquoise?"

"The flooding's so fierce it washes big rocks and everything down from the mountains. Sometimes, chunks of turquoise come too. I found a piece once – real pretty. I sold it to a dealer in Albuquerque to help pay for my wedding dress. That was a waste of money." She shook her head.

And after the floods, the turquoise just lies there, Angel realized as he put the last of the dishes away – just lies there – waiting for someone to find it. And Angel would. He'd find more. A lot more. And too bad about King Hydemann.

After that, whenever he could, Angel slipped away from the motel to hunt for turquoise. A sense of purpose fizzed through him, letting him ignore Gary's bad humor and the casual taunts of the kids at school. Celsa seemed to have decided they were going to be friends, and stopped any teasing that might have gone too far. Angel was grateful because it gave him the peace of mind to begin a plan.

The first week he'd found two more stones lying in the dust like someone had dropped them there just for him. Then a series of early storms broke over the mountains and the arroyos roared with muddy water. It was so bad that in the next town, water streamed though the main street and flooded the businesses. The following day, the newspaper printed a photo of people paddling a canoe to the grocery store. School was cancelled for a week.

With the arroyos flooded, Angel searched the high ground. Nothing. Except when he was out there, the anger and resentment the years had stacked up in his soul began to chip and crack. He watched lizards and small animals go about their business, gloried in the high wheeling flight of the desert birds. At first he fought the new feelings, but the peace of the tumbled landscape and the achingly blue sky entranced him. Day after day, the fever to be in the desert was growing on him, calling him. When he couldn't wander the hills, he read about the desert.

Celsa, seemed to know all about the land around them. She laughed at him, glancing back over her shoulder to see if he was watching while she walked away. She introduced him to the school library where he sought out information about geology, plants and animals of the area.

Gradually the water dried out, leaving even the arroyos parched and dusty despite the plants that had lunged into life with the rainfall. Then they dried out too. School ended for the summer, and Angel had nowhere to go and no one to see. Celsa helped at a tourist store in town, and he had made no other friends. He wrote two letters to his mom at the state hospital, but no answers came back.

So, he did the chores set for him by Treese and Gary, looking constantly for slivers of time to escape into the desert. His dreams at night sharpened into visions of himself free in the desert, running and hunting like one of its creatures, finding huge stones and boulders of sky blue turquoise. Throwing them against the hospital walls until they crumbled and his mother escaped.

Made wary by Celsa's stories, Angel avoided the arroyos that snaked toward Hydemann's ranch house. But weeks had passed and he hadn't found any more turquoise near the motel. Desperate, one Saturday morning, Angel had decided to search all the way down the biggest arroyo – the one that curved back toward the distant ranch buildings.

The dry streambed was steep-banked and uneven from crumbled soil and weathered rock. He had been slipping and sliding over loose stones for about an hour, when on the bank right above his head, he'd heard men's voices – ranch hands from the big house.

"Hey! You! Kid! What you doin' here!"

He'd stared up the bank at them – three men, weather-beaten and muscular. They were laughing but it was a harsh sound. The youngest one, a blonde, mustached bully, smacked his fist against his hand and called "Hey there, buddy. You're trespassing on private land. Come on up here, kid!"

Angel looked around desperately – the bank behind him was too steep. If he tried to escape that way, the men would be on him before he could get up the other side. Fear roared in his ears, pounding... *pounding...drums pounding in his ears...*

The men had started sliding down the bank toward him. "Hey you!

You're in big trouble! You're gonna have to pay for it, kid!"

Pounding...drums pounding...

Would they catch him? Tie him up? Beat him up?

Angel tried to dodge, but the men blocked him, front and back.

"Sorry, *niño*," the leader mocked, "but you gotta face the medicine!"

Breath coming in short sharp gasps, fists clenched to try and fight back, Angel tried not to imagine how much he was about to get hurt.

"Come on then! I ain't scared of you!" He hated how his voice wavered. Hated how weak he felt. All the frustration burned in his belly, burning and searing…. His rage at the hopelessness of his life roared up through him like a hot desert wind, blinding him. All around the breeze was growing stronger, bending down thin branches, raising choking dust. A storm of desert dust devils whirled down the arroyo, surrounding the ranch hands, driving clouds of sand and dirt into their eyes and mouths.

Shocked by his luck, Angel hesitated only a moment, then squeezing his eyes nearly shut against the dust, dove through the clouds and ran. While the ranch hands coughed and cursed, Angel scrambled up the bank and wove like a jack rabbit between juniper scrub and cholla cactus until the men were out of sight.

He had kept low and kept running until, heart nearly bursting, he had crawled into the hot shade of the shed. Knowing what Gary would do to him if the rancher complained, Angel had hidden there for over an hour. After that, he spent days in gut-clenched fear.

But nothing had happened – maybe the men didn't know who he was, or didn't report the incident, or maybe the rancher didn't bother. Angel didn't care why. For a week he stayed close to the motel. But the desert was calling him, seeping like dust into his skin and bones until he felt like someone new altogether. When he glanced in the mirror as he brushed his teeth or combed back his hair, his eyes seemed to have changed color, turning a clearer, more vibrant blue, but maybe that was just the desert light.

Unable to stay away from the rolling landscape, he became careful, so careful that no one ever saw him. Like the desert animals with their camouflaged colors, he learned to hold still, fade back – become invisible. In the month since school ended, he found three more nuggets. No matter how long it took, Angel had promised himself wouldn't give up until he had enough gemstones to sell to the Albuquerque dealers for the money needed to buy better medical treatment for his mom.

Afraid of Gary somehow finding out what he was doing and preventing because of sheer meanness, Angel had even created this tiny hideout. Shifting a little, Angel leaned back against the rock slab and stared longingly at the distant blue mountains. Up there, John Hydemann's mines yielded silver, copper and the finest turquoise in the state. Out of reach.

Narrowing his eyes against the wavering heat, Angel decided that tomorrow he'd get up early, do his chores and head out once Gary went into town to hang out with his buddies.

Angel rewrapped the stones and pushed them far back into the crevice. Leaning against the boulder with his knees pulled up, he relaxed into utter stillness. His worried thoughts trickled away, letting awareness of the desert life rise up around him. A road runner rattled through the dry brush. A beetle trundled past his sneakers. A coyote trotted by not fifteen feet from where he sat.

Angel's eyes drifted shut. Unaware, his hand crept up and grasped the turquoise talisman. Over the little noises of scrabbling desert life, he heard the voice. Ancient. Commanding.

"Come to us, Angel," it breathes.

"Yes, grandfather," Angel whispers.

He feels himself rise to his feet and run like the antelope across the desert, miles and miles. All around him he hears the voices of his brothers, but he can't see them. He runs and runs, beyond the arroyo, up into the hills, into a deep hidden canyon.

The sun sets and the moon shines silver across the honeycombed face of the cliff. The voice urges Angel up rough stone steps, onto the roof of the kiva. Cleansing smoke billows around the ladder that leads from the roof down into the sacred building. For a moment Angel hesitates, gazing down into the shadows, bemused by the wash of smell and sound. He coughs as he breathes in a puff of smoke from the central fire below.

"Come..."

He grasps the rounded poles and climbs down the ladder. Light flickers across the people who are waiting with whispers and low laughs for the ceremony to begin. Angel can see their shapes and movements, smell the pungency of close-packed bodies, hear excited giggles from children, see gleams of firelight on turquoise jewelry adorning the elders. But all the faces remain in shadow.

"Come," the ancient voice commands.

"Yes, grandfather," Angel whispers again. He takes his place among the shadowy people as masked dancers weave snake-like through the smoky air.

Angel's eyes turn to the grandfather. His fine white shirt gleams with heavy turquoise jewelry. His white hair is twined with eagle feathers and blue beads. But the firelight does not reach his face, leaving it in shadow.

Then the movement of the dancers draws Angel's eyes back to the celebration. First a man and woman whirl about, clutching and twisting. Then a dancer with a coyote mask circles them, arms beckoning. The first two dancers fall in behind him. Sun and moon dancers join the swirling, pounding rhythms. But the man and woman still follow Coyote who leads them away.

The snake dancers enter again and begin a long undulating dance around the kiva. Coyote darts in and out, looking sly and stealthy. Some of the children scream in excitement. Coyote pounces and draws off two snake dancers. The rest writhe in rage, stamping and shaking winged shoulders.

"Run, Coyote!" shrieks a child on Angel's left. Angel turns to look at him but he has turned too and is again lost in shadow. All the people shout encouragement to Coyote, now dashing about the kiva with his two snake children. The dance becomes wild then, with more dancers and characters than Angel can follow. The drumming pounds into his heart, his breathing, his blood. Like those around him he leaps up to take part in the wild chase.

He grabs for Coyote's tail. As his fingers brush the prickly fur, the world spins away...

FOUR

Angel's eyes flew open. It came like a physical shock to see the blazing desert around him instead of the smoky kiva. His breath whistled between his teeth and he scrubbed at his eyes with both fists. It wasn't some weird vision – he'd fallen asleep, that's all. Gary's talk about fixing up the motel with an Anasazi theme had given him dreams about the ancient pueblo Indians.

He shoved the talisman back under his shirt.

An hour later, when Angel loped back to the motel, Gary's pick-up was gone. He heaved a sigh of relief and came in through the screen door to the kitchen. Treese was there, slicing tomatoes, bread, and cheese on the cracked linoleum counter. He breathed in the smells of Treese's lavender soap, overlaid with desert dust and the sweet tang of tomato adrift in the room.

"Want a sandwich?" she asked without looking up.

"Yeah…please," Angel answered. "I'm starved."

"So what else is new?" She tipped the cheese onto a piece of crusty bread and then flipped a couple of thick tomato slices on top of that.

"Salt?" she asked.

"Sure," Angel said. "Want me to get us some Cokes?"

"Hmm," she answered.

Taking that for a yes, Angel went out into the front office where Gary kept an old cooler stocked with soft drinks for the guests. The pop cost a dollar but saying that Angel earned it, Treese had shown him a trick – a whack at the top of the door at the same time as the handle was wrenched, popped the lock. It worked every time. Angel grabbed two cold cans and then pushed the door shut.

Gary never noticed that pop was missing. Angel and Treese made sure he never saw them take a can. Every couple of weeks Treese would hand her foster son some quarters, and while Gary eyed him suspiciously from the front counter, Angel would buy a can the regular way. His foster father never caught on. For all his big shot talk, Angel suspected Gary didn't have much in the way of brains.

When Angel returned to the kitchen, a neatly cut sandwich was set at his place at the table. He slid a Coke onto the counter beside Treese. She picked it up and held it for a moment against her cheek. Angel wondered if Gary had slapped her, but he couldn't tell because Treese ate her sandwich standing up, looking out the window.

They ate in silence. When he was done, Angel carried his plate to the sink.

"Anything need doing?" he asked, glancing up under his lashes. Sure enough, Treese had a wide red mark on her face.

Anger boiled up in him again. "He shouldn't hit you!" He muttered. "Why do you let him get away with it?"

Treese eyed him measuringly. "I'm okay, Angel."

"You ought to pay him back. Bullies shouldn't get away with it… shouldn't…" Angel looked away. It wasn't his fault Gary had cracked her one, but he felt guilty anyway. Dumb, he thought. Even by wishing as hard as he could on his dragon talisman, he couldn't cause an accident. And even if he had, it wasn't his fault that Gary took it out on Treese.

"I didn't get to number 16," she said. "And I think those boys might have made some mess. Wouldn't mind some help on it. I left the cart by number 12."

Angel nodded and without meeting her eyes went into the linen room off the kitchen and took a stack of clean towels and sheets. The cart with the cleaning supplies, plastic cups and so on was waiting on the boardwalk in front of the long, single-storey wing of motel rooms. He used the master key to open up number16 and then snorted in disgust. Treese was right. The three men had left some mess. Empty beer cans and pizza boxes littered the room. One of the ash trays had been spilled into the sheets leaving a smear of scorched brown and black.

"Too bad they didn't burn the place down," Angel said aloud as he tore the stained sheets off the bed. But then he clamped his lips shut.

Be careful what you wish for, his mom had told him a long time ago. *Because you just might get it.*

Angel didn't want the motel to burn down. If it did, the social workers would move him somewhere else. He didn't much like Gary, but there were worse people out there. And Treese was nice most of the time. Besides that…Angel dropped the clean sheets on the mattress and went to the open window…out here was the desert. The desert felt like his home, something he hadn't felt in a long time. Like the place he should be. Just him and dry rocks and turquoise sky.

Angel swayed as his eyes half-closed…*wheeling up and up on the currents of air, higher than the eagles, looking down at the golden landscape rippling below the shadow of his great beating wings…*

"Look at this, then!" Treese's voice snapped Angel awake. She held up the scorched sheet. "I suppose I can bleach and then mend it, but I wish we could just turn away trash like those boys. Don't know how Gary thinks we can improve the place if folks keep wrecking it." She shook her head, took out the cleaning spray and a handful of rags, and headed to the bathroom.

"Oh, Lord!" she exclaimed. "Why couldn't they have got to the toilet if they was gonna be sick? I tell you Angel, I think we need to rethink our lives here. Whaddya say we go to Hollywood and become TV stars?"

Angel grinned, picked up a cloth and swiped the bureau. "Nah. I'm going to Cape Canaveral and become an astronaut. I want to fly up to the moon."

"Just take me with you, kid," Treese said. "'Cause I don't want to spend my life doing this every day…"

Gary didn't show up until after dinner. Angel and Treese had looped the curtain back that separated the living quarters from the front office, partly to catch any breeze, and partly to keep an eye open for customers while they watched TV. They didn't hear Gary's truck over the sound of the show, so when Angel's foster father strode in the office door, they both jumped. Gary was dirty and grinning. Angel stayed really still and cautiously breathed deeply, tasting the air for the smell of liquor. Nothing. Whatever Gary'd been up to, it hadn't happened in a bar.

"Any food around this place?" he demanded, rounding the counter into the back.

"There's some macaroni and cheese left," Treese said heaving up from the broken sofa. "That okay or you want me to thaw a hamburger?"

"Get me a burger," Gary said. He plunked down in the place Treese had vacated, picked up the remote and started switching through channels. Angel leaned away wondering if he could slide out. He didn't trust Gary's really good moods because they all too often flip-flopped into really bad ones.

His foster father switched off the TV and followed Treese into the kitchen. "You know how I got plans, Treese?" he said.

"Yeah, Gary." Treese dropped the frozen burger onto the hot pan. The scorching sizzle smoked upward into the air.

"Well, what do you think of this?" From his pocket he pulled out a handful of raw turquoise chunks and spilled them on the table. The sky blue sheen seemed to Angel to quiver in the air. He left the sofa and went to the stones as if drawn by a magic cord. When he reached out to touch the largest nugget, one half the size of his fist, Gary smacked his hand away.

"Don't you be touching those if you know what's good for you," he growled. He turned back to Treese who was staring open-mouthed. "And there's more, Treese. There's a whole lot more. These are just a start. We're gonna be rich!"

Angel stared at the stones. He'd never seen such big ones. Hardly ever seen any of such a pure blue color. His own hard-earned cache was pitiful beside these.

Treese reached out a finger to touch the largest stone. Gary stepped closer but he was grinning again, and didn't push his wife away. "Impressed, babe?"

Treese licked her lips. "You didn't...steal 'em, did you, Gary?"

"No, I didn't steal 'em. I mined 'em." Gary fetched a metal box from under the office counter, then scooped the stones up and locked them in the box. He made a show of spinning the combination. "I tell you, Treese, I'm on the edge of findin' the mother lode on these stones. It's just a matter of time, babe. And we are on our way to the big time. Hey there, Angel. Root beer all 'round to celebrate!" He handed Angel a handful of coins and sat in one of the kitchen chairs, leaning back and still grinning.

In the office, Angel looked over his shoulder, counted out three dollars and pocketed it. He whacked the pop machine and helped himself to three cans.

He put the root beers on the kitchen table and held out a few nickels and dimes. "Here's your change, Gary. Thanks."

"My pleasure, little man. You stick with me and there'll be better than root beer around here. How's my burger comin'?"

"Nearly done, Gary," Treese said from the stove. "But I just don't see where you could get turquoise like that around here. Did you...did you stake a claim in the back country?"

"Sure, me an' all them old hippies," Gary snorted. "That's pickin's for losers." He took a long swig of soda. "I did a little prospectin' up the mesa."

Treese turned around then. "But Gary, that's Hydemann's land. He prosecutes anyone that trespasses, let alone prospects. You know that, Gary. How you gonna make anything stealing from Mr. Hydemann?"

"Didn't he just about run me over today? He owes me and it's gonna cost him. I got a plan. In fact," Gary grinned, sat forward in the chair and patted the metal box, "I got a couple of plans that involve Mr. Hydemann and all his money."

Treese put his dinner in front of him. "It's gonna cost you if you steal from Hydemann."

Gary crashed his fist down on the table. "It ain't stealin'. It's prospecting. And what gives Mr. John Hydemann the right to own all that land? Is he better'n me?" He glared sullenly at Treese. "Get me some ketchup."

When she set the bottle down in front of him, Gary shook it out hard, like his hand was around someone's throat. He abruptly turned to Angel. "What do you think, boy? You think he should get it all? Or are you happy to be nothin' and have nothin' your whole life while some greedy ranch owner like Mr. John Hydemann lords it over everything?" He glared a moment at the ketchup bottle. "You know why your mom is still in that nut house? It's because the rich folks run the medical system."

"Let up, Gary," Treese interrupted.

Gary ignored her. "Angel, if you had money for medicine and treatments, you can bet your mama would be cured quick as summer lightning. You think John Hydemann's mom would ever be in a nut ward? No, sir! He's got all that cattle and mining money, so his mom would get treatments. But not your mother. You get to be a Ward...Of... The...State... because you and your mama are poor white trash and she has the misfortune to be crazy as a mad dog to boot."

"She is not!" Angel yelled.

Treese's strong arm caught him around the middle and held him. "Angel, you get on to bed." She hauled the boy a few steps down the narrow hall and all but threw him through the door into his tiny bedroom. "Go to bed," she repeated and pulled the door shut.

"No hard feelings, kid!" Gary called. Angel kicked the wall when he heard Gary laugh, and then threw himself on the bed.

He gripped the sheets and clenched his teeth so he wouldn't cry. He hated Gary. He hated John Hydemann. If Angel had turquoise he could buy better medicine and treatments for his mom. She wouldn't be crazy any more. She would stop telling people that her husband was a desert spirit named Nah-chu-ru…would forget the craziness…would get a job and a place to live…would set it up nice with a comfy sofa and bright curtains. And she'd remember she had a boy waiting for her. She'd tell people about her terrific son. She would bring her Angel home.

FIVE

The wild mood swept through Angel again next morning. The sun pulsed on his skin; the breeze brought smells he had never been aware of before – sweet cactus flowers, coyote musk, dry desert grit stirred up by dust devils whirling across parched lands. He longed to be out there, to climb high and higher up the weathered rocks until he stood with the scorching wind and hot sun beating against his chest…

Angel shook his head. He had three more rooms to clean. Treese was laid out with a migraine and Gary was in a mood of his own. If he got the rooms done quickly, maybe Gary would forget about him and he could slip away into the desert. He played with the idea of staying out all night. He'd love the feel of the velvety dark…the piercing gleam of starlight…the rustle of the small animals…

"Knock it off, Angel!" he ordered himself. This was a great way to get a whaling from Gary. He squirted a spray of bathroom cleaner into the air and let the pungent odor clear his head. The sight of Gary strolling down the motel boardwalk toward him cleared his mind even further.

"How long before the rooms are done?" Gary demanded.

"About an hour. Maybe two if they're a mess," Angel answered.

Gary stood watching, hands in his pockets, scowling. "Well, hurry up then. You and me are gonna visit Mr. Hydemann."

Angel froze. "We are? Why? And why are you taking me?"

"Just do what you're told." Gary picked up an armful of towels and a bottle of cleaning spray. "I'll do number four. You get moving on seven and eight."

Angel nodded, took the rags and went to work. He felt feverish with the need to get out into the desert, away from Gary and the motel. But, he realized as he bundled soiled linen into the cart, it didn't look like it would happen today. And *why* did Gary want him along so badly?

Whatever it was, Angel knew already he didn't want to do it. But what difference would *that* make.

Gary didn't tell him what he had in mind until they were bouncing along the highway in the old truck. Cross country, Hydemann's ranch house was about three miles from the Lone Butte Motel. By road it was nearer seven.

"Why are we going to Hydemann's ranch?" Angel asked finally. "Is it about the turquoise?"

Gary shoved Angel in the shoulder, hard. "You even mention turquoise and I'll tell your social worker you stole from the till. You know what that means?"

Angel nodded sullenly. It was a threat Gary had used before. Angel was about sure that foster kids who stole got sent to juvenile jail. There weren't enough foster homes as it was for kids like him. Throw in an accusation for theft, even if it was a lie, and that would end it for him. Angel was certain that if they locked him up away from the desert, he'd die. Die for sure. "I'm not going to say anything," he muttered.

"Good. You remember that." There was silence for a few minutes. Angel leaned his head out the open window and breathed in the hot desert smell. Off in the far distance a thunderstorm was shooting darts of lightning at a mountainside. The storm looked like a big mushroom with its column of rain in the center and the black puffy cloud spreading across the sky. A Navajo kid at school had told the class that that was the home of the Thunderbird.

"You're like a dog with its head hanging out the window." Gary drummed his fingers on the steering wheel. "Now listen, boy. My neck and back's been hurting bad since Mr. Hydemann ran me over with his big, fancy car, right in my own parking lot. I can't hardly work because of it. So's I thought I'd go ask him for a little something for doctor bills and maybe some cash settlement to help with the other bills while I'm recuperating. He's got to see I got responsibilities to my family, so I know he'll do the right thing. You understand that, boy?"

"Yeah, sure." Angel stared out at the desert. He smiled bitterly thinking about Gary's responsibilities – drinking with his buddies, yelling at him and Treese, and talking big to anyone who'd listen. He wondered if King Hydemann would catch on to what his money was supposed to help out with.

"And me?" Angel asked.

Gary chuckled. "You just stand around and look sad, boy. You are my big responsibility."

Hydemann's ranch was reached by driving through a high arched gate set in two fieldstone pillars. *Turquoise Hill Ranch* was spelled out in iron letters, all twined with some kind of winged lizards. The truck bounced through so fast, Angel didn't have a chance to see it properly.

They drove about another two miles up a long driveway. A field of feed corn edged with irrigation lines stretched off to the left. Gleaming white horse fences bounded the right side. Angel craned his neck to see a dozen beautiful animals resting in the shade of some cottonwoods. How did the rancher get enough water to keep the trees so big and healthy? He guessed Gary was right – if you had enough money, you could have anything you wanted. Even water in the desert.

They passed leafy apple trees planted amid rows of windmills. The lazily turning blades showed Angel where the Turquoise Hill Ranch got its power for lights and, most important, for pumping water into the fields. Angel spied black solar panels fitted onto the roofs of the farm buildings.

Gary slowed down the truck when they passed a dozen peach trees. "Just figure what it'd be like to have your own peaches fresh off a tree," he commented. "Me though, I'd try for some cherries too." For a moment he stared out at the branches loaded with hard green fruit, nodding in the endless wind. "Sure hope this ain't all ruined for Mr. John Hydemann by some hail storm." He yanked the truck into gear again.

The house wasn't as big as Angel had thought it would be. After all Celsa had said, Angel had expected at least a palace. Instead, John Hydemann's home was a sprawling stucco bungalow with arched columns supporting red tiled roofs over shady porches. Flower gardens bright with roses and other blooms surrounded the house. More usual cactus gardens stretched along the paths that led to the barns, garages and houses for the ranch workers. Angel craned his neck to see if he could spot his friend. There was no sign of her, just an old, white dog ambling toward the shade of a tree.

"They got a lot of water?" he asked Gary.

His foster father nodded. "A branch of the Jemez River runs through here. That's why the ranch can keep so many head of cattle. It's not much more than a creek over there…" he gestured to the line of trees in the horse pasture, "but it's enough and it don't run dry." He sighed. "I sure would've liked to have a Daddy that left me a place like this. All I got was the motel and I got that by marryin' Treese. Sure don't seem fair."

"Nope," Angel agreed.

Gary turned and punched him lightly on the arm. "But men of enterprise can move up in the world anyway, right boy? Let's go start on our fortune."

When the truck door slammed, a small, dark-haired woman bustled out onto the porch. "*Buenos dias*," she said. "Can I help you?"

"I'm here to see Mr. Hydemann," Gary said.

"Is he expecting you?" The woman cocked her head, eyes running over Gary's beat up truck and their worn clothes.

"No, but I got some business with him, if he's available." Gary smiled, looking sure of himself. Angel felt his own face flush, so he looked around at the flowers instead. The scent of them floated everywhere. Angel breathed deeply and his nostrils somehow separated each of the individual scents. The rich heavy perfume had to be that velvet red rose…the sharp, candy-light tang came from the small purple flowers – he was sure of it. Without realizing he turned and began walking toward the flowers. And another smoky-sweet aroma rose over the whole, quickening his heartbeat…

"Angel!" Gary's voice broke the spell. "Come say *Hi* to Mr. Hydemann."

Reluctantly Angel turned and mounted the steps to the porch. He kept his head down when Mr. Hydemann offered them seats around a glass table. The rancher sat facing them, arm stretched out across the back of his chair. "So, what can I do for you, Mr. Tanner?"

"Gary…call me Gary."

"Well then, Gary, what can I do for you?" Angel had the feeling that Mr. Hydemann's voice was less friendly than it had been the day before. He guessed the rancher wouldn't be smiling at him any more, and for some reason that made him feel sad, like the chance for something important had been lost. Angel scowled. Maybe he had been spending too much time in the desert after all, and the heat was cooking his brains.

"Well, you see, John," Gary was saying, "it's like this. I woke up this morning feeling like someone had put my neck and back on a roller coaster, and it didn't do them no good neither."

"Hmmm…" Mr. Hydemann murmured.

"I went and saw my doctor this morning…" Angel looked up in surprise. Gary hadn't left the motel. "…and he said I got to rest up for two…three weeks. Maybe even a month to avoid some permanent injury."

"I see," Mr. Hydemann said.

"Now, I got responsibilities, I told the doctor," Gary leaned forward toward the rancher. Angel twisted farther away as though he could completely distance himself from his foster father. "I got a motel to run, a wife and family…" he gestured toward Angel. "I can't just stop being a Daddy because I got hurt. I mean, me and Angel had plans to go hiking and camping. I hate to disappoint my boy." Gary heaved a sigh.

Angel stared at Gary. His foster father had never done a thing with him since he'd lived at the Lone Butte Motel. Except maybe yell and push him around.

"It must be a worry," Mr. Hydemann commented.

"Yes sir, John," Gary said sadly, "yes, it is. But my real worry is the mortgage payments…light…water…and of course," he paused, "all those doctor bills. All that from a few seconds of your car runnin' into me in my own parking lot."

"Yes, I see," Mr. Hydemann said. "What do you think would ease that worry, Mr. Tanner?"

Gary smiled. "I think a wealthy man like you might feel just a little responsible for my difficulties."

Angel fixed his eyes on his worn sneakers. Bouncing along the road in Gary's truck, it had seemed like a good idea to ask Mr. Hydemann for money. But he hadn't known Gary would lie so much. And the lies made him feel dirty and small.

"Do you think two thousand dollars would ease your worries, Mr. Tanner?" Angel heard the flint in Mr. Hydemann's voice.

"Not as much as three thousand would," Gary shot back.

The woman they had seen first came out onto the porch carrying a tray with tall glasses and a pitcher of iced tea. Celsa followed with a plate of cookies. Angel's eyes flew to her face, and then his cheeks burned with shame at the con Gary had sucked him into.

"Here's some tea for your guests, *señor* Hydemann," she said.

"Celsa, just put the tray on the table."

"What are you doing here?" Celsa hissed at Angel as she set down the tray. He could smell some kind of flower scent swirling around her, and her skin looked warm and silky. He felt his face get hotter still; his mouth opened and shut soundlessly like some stupid fish thrown into the dirt.

"Thank you, Ana...Celsa," Mr. Hydemann said.

"*De nada*," Ana said. "Celsa, come help me fix lunch."

Following her mother into the house, Celsa glanced back, frowning. Angel dropped his gaze to his twisting fingers and silently hated Gary... and himself.

The rancher gestured toward the plate. "Help yourself, Mr. Tanner and...?" He glanced toward Angel.

"Look at Mr. Hydemann," Gary ordered as he reached for the cookies.

Angel lifted his head so that his eyes met Mr. Hydemann's. He saw the rancher's brows rise.

"What's your name, son?" Mr. Hydemann asked.

"That's my boy, Angel," Gary interrupted, talking over a mouthful of cookie crumbs. "Weird name, but that's what his Mama chose. Not even the Mexican way of saying it...*Ahn–gale*..." He took a long drink of iced tea.

Mr. Hydemann looked sharply at Gary. "Your son's eyes are a very different color than yours, Mr. Tanner."

Gary shrugged. "I don't know nothin' about genetics. I guess he got them somewhere's, hey?"

Mr. Hydemann stood up. "Yes, I guess he did. Let's get on with our business." He went into the house.

Gary looked after the rancher with a satisfied smirk and poured himself another full glass of iced tea, careless of the splashes he left behind.

"This here's somethin' like." He leaned back and gazed out over the property as though he himself was master of the land. Angel twisted in his chair to stare off at the mountains. He could have been out there in the desert, not listening to Gary's lies or having Hydemann stare at him. Why should the rancher pay any attention to his eyes? So what if they were a weird color? His mother had told him they were the same as his father's eyes. Too bad she had told him that in front of the doctors, then kept on going to say her husband was a desert spirit – a blue one, for Pete's sake.

"Hey Angel, try one of these cookies." Gary reached for another.

Angel ignored him. His hand crept to the talisman under his shirt. Eyes the color of desert sky and a chunk of carved turquoise – that was all he'd gotten from his father.

He would have done better if Gary really was his old man…

SIX

"So then I talked him up to three thousand dollars," Gary bragged to Treese a couple of hours later over lunch. He bit into his thick bacon sandwich and chewed thoughtfully. "But the way I see it, he still owes me."

"I don't think Mr. Hydemann will see it that way at all," Treese said. She was still heavy-eyed from her headache and didn't seem very happy about the extra money.

Angel decided not to mention that when Mr. Hydemann finally came back onto the porch he'd carried a fancy leather-bound check book and a crisp file folder with papers his lawyer had faxed over for Gary to sign. Mr. Hydemann made it real clear that once Gary wrote his name on those papers, he had sworn that the three thousand was enough and he wouldn't try for more money. Angel had hidden a smile by wiping his mouth on his arm. Gary hadn't liked that at all, but he'd had no choice, not if he wanted the check Mr. Hydemann wrote out to him.

Then Mr. Hydemann had offered Angel some more cookies and when the boy turned them down, the rancher had walked them to the old truck.

"Treated me good," Gary gloated later to Treese.

Angel took another bite of his sandwich. He thought it was more like Mr. Hydemann was making sure they got off his property.

The mid-day heat was a killer today, so Treese went back to bed. Angel heard her switch on the wheezy old fan. The air conditioning in the living quarters had been broken for a couple of months. As he cleared off the table and washed the dishes, Angel wondered if Gary would use some of the money to fix the air conditioning or if he'd blow it on something dumb. While Angel cleaned up, Gary lounged on the sofa, flicking TV channels. He must've still been feeling good about the check because he treated Angel to a root beer when he got one for himself.

Then his foster father unlocked the safe and took out his metal box of turquoise. He smoothed a white towel over the kitchen table, and then made a big show of hiding the combination that unlocked the box. Angel slouched against the wall, faking indifference, but all the while feeling an increased thrumming of his heart at the nearness of the turquoise. As Gary spilled out the stones, they pooled on the white cloth like broken pieces of sky. Even the soft, reddish matrix stone that surrounded some of the nuggets couldn't hide the pure color of the turquoise. Angel's breath caught in his throat with longing – longing like homesickness and missing his mom and running free in the desert, all mixed up together.

"That check from Hydemann is three thousand, and I bet there's another ten thousands' worth here..." Gary was saying. "You never seen so much all in one place, have you Angel."

Angel shook his head. "No," he said slowly. "Where'd you find it, Gary? You want me to come help you? You can mine out more that way. I'd work hard for just a bit of it..."

Gary's hand shot out, aiming to slap the boy. The man's face twisted into a snarl even as Angel ducked out of the way. "This here's my treasure and my find! Don't you even think about it. I ain't takin' you with me so's you can spill my secret. And none of this is for you, neither. You understand that!"

"But Gary," Angel pleaded, but still keeping the kitchen table between them, "you can mine twice as much if I help. And I won't tell nobody. Gary, if I had some, just a little, I could get those treatments for my mom. Think about it, Gary! You could get twice as much and it'd only cost you a little for my mom." Angel stared into Gary's face hopefully. "Please, Gary. You know how hard I can work..."

Gary laughed, not a nice sound. "You'll keep doin' the work around here," he said. "Or we'll dump you back on the state. And they don't want you neither. There ain't no other place for you anywhere. You just don't know when you're well off, that's all."

Sullen resentment blew through Angel again, making him long for the muscles and maybe just the courage to pound the sneer from Gary's face. Make him beg. "It's for my mom," Angel repeated.

Gary shrugged, gathered the stones back up, and locked them in the box. "We all got our troubles, boy. And I don't see how yours or your mom's are my worry." He took the box and locked it into the safe. "I'm going into town to cash this check," he called over his shoulder. "Tell Treese I won't be home to eat. I'm gonna celebrate!"

Angel stood without moving until he heard Gary's truck cough into gear and the uneven rumble of its engine had faded into the desert silence. His heart was pounding, his breath whistling in his throat as much as if he'd been running to escape Gary's blows. He leaned against the table, searching the surface for even a grain of the rock to have been left behind. Nothing. Nothing but the feel of Gary's meanness in the heavy air.

And behind that, his own helpless rage. Building. Climbing higher. Bubbling up into his mind from deep inside.

He's listening to the radio, singing along...already forgetting his "responsibilities" back at the motel. Angel's fury trails him like clouds of grey-blue exhaust fumes...billowing behind...

"This here's one lucky, lucky cowboy..." Gary yodels.

Angel's anger swarms forward in clouds of grey dust, coating the truck, hiding the road...

A horn honks wildly.

Gary curses, yanks the wheel...the truck bounces hard as the wheels hit the rough shoulder. The tires skid on the slope of the ditch...Gary yells, yanks the wheel again...

"No!" Angel gasped. He shook his head like a dog, trying to shake off the lingering drops of fury. He wasn't going to go crazy like his mom. He wouldn't go off into dreams like her. It didn't matter how much of a jerk Gary was; Angel wasn't going to be driven by him or anyone into craziness.

With shaking hands he poured himself a glass of water and gulped it down. It was too bad Mrs. Preston, the social worker, was never around when Gary got to slapping. She wasn't due to show up for another three days, when she'd drive Angel to Albuquerque for his monthly visit to his mom.

What if Angel did tell the social worker about Gary's bullying? He knew what would happen then – the state agency would take Angel away from the motel and find somewhere else for him to live. Maybe. If there was a place anywhere. He'd stayed in a lot of dreary places since his mom got too sick to look after him, and all things considered, this was the best. The desert was all around him, and the desert made up for almost everything.

The desert. Out there, he could be calm. Out there, he could find turquoise.

Moving quietly, so as not to wake Treese, Angel went into his room hauled out his back pack and dumped the junk left from the end of the school year onto his bed. He took socks, underwear, and a hooded sweatshirt from his dresser and shoved them into the empty bag. Rooting in the bottom of the closet, he found his shoebox of personal stuff. Mixed in with photos of him and his mom, an old birthday card and some glittery rock, lay a fat pocket knife left behind by a trucker the month before. That went into his pocket.

Taking his pack, he went back into the kitchen. A quick survey turned up two oranges, a box of crackers and the fried chicken left from Sunday dinner. Angel folded the tinfoil back and sniffed the batter coated chicken. His mom had made great fried chicken. Better than anyone else's he'd ever tasted. Even when they had almost no money, she could make food taste good.

"All in the seasoning and then cookin' it just right – not too fast and not too slow," she'd told him.

"Cookin' it ju-u-ust right," Angel had chorused. He'd been a lot younger then, still full of jokes and laughs.

"Ju-u-ust right." She'd grinned back at him. He remembered her big crooked teeth – a poor woman's smile, but he loved it.

Her smiles had been gone for a few years now. Sometimes Angel believed he'd never see them again.

Scowling, he pressed the foil back over the chicken and pushed it into his pack. He hoped it didn't leak onto his socks. From the cooler he took two cans of root beer and two bottles of water and shoved them in the pack as well. At the last minute, he crossed to the coat rack for the stained cowboy hat that Treese had given him, and crammed it onto his head.

Before heading out, he scribbled a note for Treese:

Gary's eating in town. I'm going camping in the desert. Back tomorrow.
– Angel

"There," he said. "This'll be that hiking trip you told old Hydemann about."

He swung the backpack over his shoulders, pushed through the screen door, headed across the parking lot and jumped the leaning wire fence onto Hydemann land. Feeling the hot wind in his face, Angel set off at a trot, leaving the Lone Butte Motel behind.

As the steady rhythm of his feet matched the beat of his heart, the motel faded into the heat haze behind him and Angel melted into the desert landscape. He ran steadily, smelling the pungent dust and faint tang of pine, rejoicing in the hot whoosh of breeze across his face and prickling of dry air in his nostrils. Swerving to avoid a snaggle of cholla cactus, he startled a small lizard into scampering off, and then jumped to one side to avoid a rattlesnake uncoiling beneath the dry brush.

"Hey there, brother, don't bite me," Angel chanted. He spread his arms and stamped his feet like the snake dancers in his dream. The freedom bursting in his heart made even the rattler his friend.

Head weaving, tail rattling slowly, the five foot diamondback peered at the dancing, flapping figure.

"Dance with me," Angel hissed. The snake lowered his head and slithered away, his scales rasping softly on the dry grass and stones.

Angel laughed, not caring that this was crazy, and using his feet to pound a rhythm danced in a circle. He had no words so he sang, "*Hey! Hey! Hey- uh hey! I fly in the sky. I soar in the blue. I am greater than the eagles...Hey! Hey! Hey- uh hey!*"

He sang and danced and pounded until the sweat ran from his forehead. He wiped it with his forearm and saw the muddy smear across his skin. Holding his face to the sun, he felt dust and heat blending into his bones.

He soared high, pure sun on his back, cool air in his face. He heard wing thrusts behind, voices calling to him..."Fly with us, brother...fly with us, my son..."

A golden eagle screamed, waking Angel from his trance. He blinked, swaying, suddenly lonely. Scanning the sky, he watched the eagle wing its way toward the mountains. It must have a nest up there, maybe a mate and fledglings. Angel wished he could see them, but wishing wouldn't do him any good. The sun would be setting in a couple of hours and he needed to find a camping spot.

Looking around him, Angel felt a flash of exasperation with himself.

Getting mad at Gary had stopped him thinking – he had not brought a blanket or even started off in the direction of his cache. The days might be hot but in the high desert the nights were often cool. His secret stash was about a half mile to the east. The canyon he wanted to search was another two miles to the west. Sometimes these days, it seemed like thinking just went out the window when he got to feeling and that scared him.

"Don't get stupid, now, Angel," he told himself sternly.

He'd seen what happened when a person gave up thinking because the feelings won out. At best, they got stupid and mean like Gary. At worst, they got sick in their minds like his mom. No matter what happened, he wasn't going to let himself get like that.

It took him about fifteen minutes to get to his hideout. With two blankets, matches, beef jerky and two more bottles of water stuffed in his pack, he was ready.

As he jogged toward the arroyo, he scanned the smoky blue mountains on the near horizon. That's where the flash floods started. Immense grey-matted clouds would drift on the high winds across the desert, then snag on the mountains. Sheeting rain would drown the slopes, streaming and flooding across the mountain faces. Then muddy torrents would roar and crash downward, gouging canyons and arroyos, spreading the life that made the desert bloom while washing away anything that got in the way.

Usually the flash floods came in late summer, not winter like a lot of places, but any freak storm could catch unsuspecting hikers, tear apart bridges or turn the roads into surging rivers. Today, though, the sky looked clear in every direction.

Angel reached the canyon in less than an hour. Stunted junipers, sharp-edged yucca, golden-flowered chamisa, and dry desert grasses lined the steeply sloped sides and tufted at the bottom. Even though he picked the easiest descent he could, Angel still ended up dusty and scratched. The dry stream bed was strewn with stones that had been shattered and tumbled by years and years of surging flood water. Big rocks lined the sides; sometimes they too had been cracked and chunks had fallen into ankle-breaking piles. Angel scanned the dusty bed, looking for the blue shimmer of turquoise. Nothing.

He hadn't expected it, really. He thought he'd have better luck higher up toward the buttes and mountains. The way the canyon split the desert floor, Angel guessed it might snake in the direction of Hydemann's ranch house, possibly intersecting with the deep rift where the ranch hands had nearly caught him a couple of months ago. Angel decided he'd follow the stream bed in the direction away from the ranch as long as the light held, then make camp in one of the narrower side canyons. This far away, he doubted any of Hydemann's ranch hands would spot him if he stayed below the horizon line.

Determined, Angel set off toward the mountains, his eyes continuously scanning for flashes of blue – the washed away leftovers from the distant mines. That was one thing Gary was right about. Hydemann didn't deserve to have it all. Not when a single handful of good turquoise could buy treatments that Angel hoped would cure his mother. Breathing steadily, Angel kept up his steady trot. He would not stop, not ever, until he had enough to save his mom.

SEVEN

As the sky melted from dusky rose to velvet blue-black, Angel made camp. Using his sweatshirt to protect his hands, he gathered the woody skeletons of dead cholla and then with dry grasses for tinder, built a small hot fire. Sitting cross-legged, eating his chicken, he wished he had proper camping gear so that he could stay out here longer. He managed to split the purple fruit of a prickly pear he had found, dug out the seedless part of the flesh, and chewed that. It was delicious.

Deep night flowed across the desert, spreading cool breezes and swishes of sound and scent. Listening to the crackle of his fire and the soft desert sounds, smelling the smoke and drifting desert perfumes, Angel felt utterly peaceful. Even the worries about his mother seemed to fade into a dreamy half-memory. Around him, the desert sang an ancient song and he was woven into the chorus. He rose gladly to the song, and in spirit ran and soared over the desert landscape. Once again he descended the ladder into the kiva.

"He returns," a voice murmurs.

"Welcome...welcome..." the voices cradle him, drawing him into the smoky sweet darkness. He takes his place in the circle as the grandfather raises his hand for silence.

The grandfather says, "Here is a story. It is the story of how Coyote's tricks led the people to this world. It is the story of how The People became the clan of the winged serpent. Listen to the story.

"When First Man and First Woman and Coyote were created, the first world was too small. And so they climbed upward into the second world where the sun, moon and stars lived. Sun fell in love with First Woman, and followed her everywhere, not caring that his scorching heat hurt her. To help First Woman escape, Coyote led her and the people of the second world upward to the third world. Here in the third world of creation, all was beautiful and peaceful. Too peaceful for Coyote the

trickster.

"*The mountain people of the third world warned the newcomers that everyone could live in peace, providing no one disturbed Tieholtsodi, the great serpent. Telling Coyote not to do something made sure that he did it, wicked Coyote!*

"*Creeping up on the great horned serpent, Coyote spied her two beautiful children. The boy child shone blue as summer sky. The girl child shimmered silver as running water. Coyote loves beauty and so he snatched the serpent's children and ran off with them.*

"*Tieholtsodi roared with fury, demanding the return of her children. Coyote ran faster. Tieholtsodi flung herself into the air and spread her eagle wings. Coyote ran faster and faster, and the snake could not catch him.*

"*In her rage, Tieholtsodi gulped in all the water of the lower worlds and spat floods after Coyote. Even then he did not return her children. As the water rose through the third world, the people had no choice but to climb higher and higher. The mountain people used their magic to pile the mountains from the four corners of the world, one on top of another. Still the water rose and still Coyote would not let go of Tieholtsodi's children. At last the people and animals had no choice but to climb a giant reed into the fourth world. Turkey was the last to leave. The water washed the tips of his tail feathers white, and they are still white to this day.*

"*The people thought they were safe, but the winged serpent fanned the waters higher and higher, until the ground of the fourth world became mud. Again the people stacked the mountains on top of one another and all the people and animals climbed a magical reed into the fifth world, the world we live in today.*

"*Tieholtsodi roared out that she would not sleep and the waters would not stop rising until her children were returned. She did not care that the children had grown up and married into the tribe – that they had children and the children had children. Time means nothing to the mother of serpents. She sent out her voice and the waters washed upward, filling the mountain with the magic of the great serpent, washing outward over the fifth world, gouging arroyos and flooding the plains. The people ordered Coyote to return Tieholtsodi's children. Coyote did so and the great serpent was satisfied.*

"The winged snake drank back the waters until the beautiful desert stretched around them and the people and animals had every food and shelter needed. From then on, the people of the fifth world and Tieholtsodi's family were one clan. So that her grandchildren would have her strength in the fifth world, she filled the mountain with her blue magic. The stones carry her magic.

"Tieholtsodi and her children returned to the third world, but I do not know if they live there still.

"That is the story."

A coyote yipped nearby, and Angel jerked upright. Once again, the dream had been so real that he could feel the heat of the people's bodies where they had pressed against him. He could smell the kiva's pluming smoke...or was it just the smell of his own campfire? He shivered and the sensations faded into the night. Angel could have cried out with the sudden loneliness.

Beyond the dim circle of firelight, a coyote's eyes briefly shone yellow. Now Angel felt the creature's aching hunger. *Hunting had not been good and there was a den of pups...*

Pulling the bones and scraps from the tinfoil, Angel threw them to the coyote. He heard the scrabble and snaps as the animal swallowed the meat and cracked the bones. "Take this for you wife and babies," he called and tossed a handful of jerky.

The fire was nearly burned down, so Angel pulled on his sweatshirt. He wrapped himself tightly in both blankets, partly for warmth as the night cooled, and partly to keep any of the desert creatures from burrowing into his blankets to seek his body warmth. Angel grinned at the thought. He was willing to dance with a rattler, but he'd rather not sleep with one.

He dropped off to sleep quickly, lulled by the cocoon of desert breezes, scents and sounds. The dreams crowded onto him – *dipping, twisting flights above weathered rock, glittering flashes of movement, drum beats and dances, cries of terror...cries of joy...*

Morning was just easing over the horizon when Angel's eyes flickered open. He took a deep shaky breath and dropped the turquoise talisman. He had been gripping it in his sleep again. Was it the cause of all these weird dreams? But they were just dreams; they couldn't be the start of crazy, could they?

He sat up, and the glory of the sunrise washed away the lingering wisps of sleep. Angel stretched, and then with his blankets still tightly wrapped around his middle, sat up. A gecko watched from a nearby rock. A dusty-backed bluebird winged by in search of breakfast.

Angel unwound his blankets enough to allow him to build another small fire. He held his hands out to the flames more for the pleasure of the scorching heat than because he was cold. Again he wished he had camping gear – a pan to fry eggs and bacon and a pot and mug so he could make coffee.

But he was happy eating his oranges and crackers, washing them down with a can of soda. He hadn't provisioned himself very well, though. He'd have to go back to the motel tonight if he wanted anything much to eat today. There was still enough water in his pack, and another half-package of crackers, but even if he found more cactus fruit it wouldn't be much.

Still, with the new sun warming his face and the company of the wildlife flitting about, Angel thought it was about as perfect as a morning could get. He sighed. Maybe if he found enough turquoise and his mom got well, they could live out here in the desert. There must be a corner of it somewhere that no one would mind them having. Even King Hydemann didn't own every foot of it.

He gathered up his litter and stuffed it in his pack. Then he kicked apart and buried the remains of his fire. When he was satisfied that he'd left no trace of his camp, he stretched, lifted up his pack, and began a slow, careful walk up the canyon.

He scanned the exposed rock and tumbled stones, looking for the telltale blue shine. Sometimes with a gasping grunt, he heaved over big rocks that looked recently deposited. Turquoise could be bleached out by sun and water, its value reduced as the color faded and the stone became crumbly. Most turquoise that the local prospectors found around here were greeny-blue veins, sandwiched in old volcanic rock. But the stones he dreamed of, the nuggets that Gary had shown him, were the sky's glowing blue with only a hint of early morning green. He imagined them roped or chunked in hidden cavities, growing and deepening in color over the centuries. And he could see and hear the crack as rock faces eroded and fell away, revealing the hidden gems – to him. To Angel who belonged to the desert.

He was so intent on his hunt, that he didn't see the rancher before he heard buzzing, rasping rattles.

Angel's head shot up. Teetering on a flat rock above the bank, flanked by cholla spines, John Hydemann was edging back from the weaving, wedged head of a seven-foot diamondback. Behind him, two more venomous snakes reared their heads, their rattles vibrating. Angel sucked in his breath. The rancher was dead for sure.

EIGHT

Rattling filled the desert air, shaking all other sounds away from Angel's ears. The rancher's eyes were intent, wary, as he shifted around on the unstable rock, trying to keep as far from the snakes as he could. He glanced up and saw Angel.

"Stay back…" Hydemann commanded in a low voice.

Angel froze. He shouldn't be here. Hydemann had caught him. If Gary knew…Angel could feel the slaps…hear the cursing…*he had to get away*…

The rattling increased in tempo. A sheen of sweat glistened on the rancher's forehead. "Don't come any closer, son," Hydemann said softly. He leapt back as the largest snakehead slashed toward him. He danced forward again, as a smaller snake reared to strike.

Angel's breath came in gasps. He had to…he had to help the rancher. His mind raced – he could run to the ranch house…get someone. But that would be too late for Hydemann. By the time they telephoned for anti-venom, by the time the men came, by the time they got him to the hospital…it would be too late. Could treatments come extra fast for a rich man? Fast enough to save him? Angel's eyes met those of the rancher's again…

Angel slipped the pack off his back and groped for the turquoise snake under his shirt.

"Grandfather," he whispered. "Help me, grandfather…"

Memory…power…throbbed in his veins, propelling him upward toward the rancher.

"Stay back, Angel!" Hydemann's voice came from far away.

Angel smelled the smoky sweet scent of the kiva, felt the pounding of dancers' feet. The shadow people wove around him again, drew him into their dance. Angel fell into the shuffle-footed rhythm of the snake dancers. He could hear their chants…knew what words to sing out…

"Brothers," he called. "My brothers…listen to a boy of your clan…"

Around him whirl the dancers of his people. Turquoise beads shine in their hair, on their wrists, against their chests. He is part of them, part of their power. The rock and snakes are shadows as Angel dances around them. He is in the kiva again, dancing the dance of the great serpent, the mother of all snakes, grandmother of his clan. As he weaves and stamps, he is aware of the surging power of the amulet pulsing on his chest. It burns through his veins, awakening him, calling him to the sky.

"Come away, cousins," he calls to the snakes. "This man is no food for your children."

The reptilian heads weave back and forth in time to his stamping feet.

"Come away, sister," he chants. "It is time to hunt in another place."

The smallest diamondback drops its head and lazily sways off into the brush.

"Come away, brothers," Angel commands. "This man will share my fire."

He nears the remaining two snakes now. His steps slow. Their beaded eyes look into his. First one and then the other drops down and winds away into the dry landscape.

Still feeling the pulsing magic of the dance, Angel slowly stops moving, then simply stands, letting his breathing ease back to normal. The dance fades, the drumming becomes an echo on the hot wind…

He was barely aware of the movement when Mr. Hydemann jumped from the rock and came toward him. Angel stared longingly up into the vast sky, ready to leap upwards, to soar in the cold thin air of the high altitudes. They called…

"How did you do that?" The rancher's voice slammed him back to earth.

Angel jerked…turned to the man he'd saved. The rancher's face was pale, damp with perspiration – but his gaze was clear and sharp.

"How did you do that?" He stepped closer and he grasped Angel's thin shoulder in a hard grip. "That language…it wasn't Zuni, Hopi or Navajo…what was it? Where did you learn it? Your mother…did she teach you?"

"Don't talk about my mother!" Angel yelled. He wrenched free and took to his heels. He had to get away from the rancher, from the new craziness that had just happened to him.

"Wait!" Hydemann called. "Angel, wait! I just want to talk to you!"

Angel didn't even turn. He tore down the bank of the arroyo, slipping and stumbling, banging his shins and scraping his hands and knees. He grabbed his pack – he had to get away.

He ran, tearing up the far bank, pounding over the baked earth, scrambling over rearing rocks, swerving past cactus, until the rancher's voice had faded and he was alone once more in the landscape. His breath came in gasps. Cool tracks on his cheeks dried in the breeze. Like one of the desert animals, he had to go to earth, to hide. Curling up in a crevice between two rocks, he tried not to think or feel.

Tried not to think what would happen if Hydemann told Gary that Angel had been trespassing in his desert. The desert where Gary was stealing Hydemann's turquoise. The desert where Angel was searching for washed out turquoise to save his mother.

Tried not to remember that he had danced a snake dance and commanded the obedience of three rattlers in some weird Indian language he didn't even know.

Tried not to wonder if he was getting crazy like his mother.

But he couldn't stop wondering, couldn't stop thinking. An hour later, with the sun at its height, he still crouched in the thin shade of a boulder. His eyes flicked over the landscape. Nothing moving but a small lizard. Could he talk to it? Could some people...not just crazy people talk to animals? He couldn't believe he had danced around three rattlesnakes.

What if Hydemann told Gary?

Was there something special about him? Something the turquoise talisman was doing to him? Or was he just getting sick in his head like his mother?

He licked his lips, dragged out a bottle of water and gulped it down. What if he started seeing spirits in the desert like she had? But all he'd had were dreams – dreams from ordinary stuff like...like Gary talking about the Anasazi. It wasn't the same.

Did his mom think she could talk to snakes?

He pulled the talisman out from under his shirt. Maybe that was the problem. Maybe the coiled, winged snake had some kind of curse on it. Were there curses? His breathing quickened. Maybe he should rip it off and fling it away into the dust.

No! He forced his mind clear and touched the carved coils. Under his fingers the cool stone arched into delicate wings and a sinuous body – and that was all. There was no surge of dreams. Nothing. He'd imagined it. Just imagined it.

And gotten really lucky with those snakes.

Angel dropped the turquoise under his shirt and took another long drink of water. Wearily, with the empty bottles stowed in his backpack and the disturbing thoughts shoved out of his head, Angel got to his feet. For a moment he wondered if he should hurry back to the motel and hope Gary hadn't noticed he was gone. Somehow, he'd have to make sure Hydemann didn't come around making trouble for him. But how?

If Gary had already noticed he'd run off, Angel had to make this trip worth something. If he was going to get slapped around by his foster father when he slunk back, he had better find some turquoise to buy those treatments for his mom. He was close to a narrow canyon he hadn't explored before, and he was not ready to give up.

"You can count on me, Mom," he said loudly. "Don't care if Hydemann comes after me. Don't care if Gary roughs me up."

He waited a minute, listening to the still air as if his mom would send back an answer. Nothing. He grinned his relief. Maybe not crazy after all.

This streambed was only a few yards across, but deep. The banks rose on either side crenellated and uneven, trapping hot air between them. Angel slid down and started hunting. Within a few minutes he found three tiny, faded nuggets. But they had been exposed to water and sun for too long. They crumbled between his fingers – worthless.

Hot wind rattled through the desert shrubs. Angel turned over rock after rock. Nothing. The sun beat down on his back; the hair under his hat was plastered to his skull. He wiped his dripping face on his shirt and bent to force up the edge of another big slab. A fist sized, reddish rock rolled out – sky blue streaked the rock face. Turquoise!

"Yeah!" Angel hissed in triumph.

Crouching, he scooped up the rock, spit on it and rubbed away the dust. Holding the stone to the light, he tilted it this way and that to highlight the blue glow. Opening his knife, Angel prodded the stone, cracking away some of the worthless matrix rock. His shoulders drooped. The turquoise wasn't much more than a splash on the stone's face.

He sat back on his heels. The shape of the gemstone fracture made it look like it had split away from a bigger vein. Angel gazed up toward the hills, following the line of the streambed, shifting his eyes to the smoky blue mountain miles back. The sacred mountain. Home of the Thunderbird. The place of ancestors. But these days nobody, not even the local Indians got to go there because Hydemann owned it. And King Hydemann didn't allow any trespassers on his land.

Angel sucked in his breath. All the Hydemann mines, though, were in the hills to the east. This turquoise had to have come from the sacred mountain – from a mountain no one mined and a deposit no one even knew about!

Angel's heartbeat sped up. He could find the turquoise! One backpack full of stones and he'd have enough to buy treatments for his Mom and get them a nice little place. She could get better! Maybe she would be cured in a couple of months. He could get her out of the hospital...they could be a family...

Angel swallowed. That mountain was miles away. He'd have to cross miles of open desert.

He had no gear...

If Gary caught him...

If Hydemann found out...

His Mom could get better...

Angel narrowed his eyes, mentally measuring the distance. It would take at least two days to hike there if he headed straight across the desert and on that landscape he'd stick out like flag on the horizon. But what if he stayed low, in the canyons by day and only in the open at night? Could he go that far? Would he dare? What if he took off and Gary tracked him down...what would his stepfather do to him?

"If you get the turquoise, it won't matter what Gary thinks," Angel whispered. But what if Hydemann caught him? Would Angel's saving him from the rattlers keep the man from sending him to jail? Maybe. But Hydemann was famous for hammering anyone who took his turquoise or trespassed too far onto his land. Why would he change for some kid – even when that kid had saved his life? Rich people didn't get rich by being fair or being nice. He had better not count on any good treatment from the rancher. And unlike Gary, he was too scared to try to take advantage of Hydemann. Angel cracked a brief smile. Maybe he was just a lot smarter than Gary when it came down to it.

For a few moments, Angel tried to figure out a way to just head out to the mountain. Back at the motel, nothing was waiting for him except a probable run-in with his foster father. But how far would he get without supplies and water? Besides, Hydemann would know that he was out here where he didn't belong and maybe his men would be watching for him. He had to wait until everyone's eyes weren't on him any longer. Seething in frustration, Angel thrust the stone into his pack, repocketed his knife and scrambled up the bank.

He hadn't gone more than a hundred yards before he saw tire tracks through flattened brush.

Hydemann's men? Or Gary's truck?

Angel's breath whistled through his gritted teeth – the same wild rage was on him again. Get a grip…Maybe they aren't Gary's tracks, Angel told himself fiercely. The ranch hands checked on cattle with trucks as well as horses, didn't they? No big deal.

But what if Gary had found his cache of turquoise in the sacred mountain? Sick with despair at the idea that Gary might have gotten to it before him, Angel set off at a run, following the tracks until they joined a kind of rough road that wound into the horizon. He stared at the tracks and the distant mountain, wanting to race after them – to find out if the wheel ruts led to turquoise.

But maybe the tracks came from the ranch. That would mean his turquoise was safe.

Now Angel raced the other way, following the tracks backward, hoping for any kind of proof that Gary had not come this way. The sun beat on his shoulders and neck, making sweat stream down his forehead and back. He paused long enough to swallow a few gulps from a water bottle. If he had any brains, he's go home before someone caught him.

No brains, Angel decided grimly and kept going.

The tire tracks led to a county road where a broken gate lay flat on the ground. The road twisted away to the highway. Angel stood before the broken gate, chest heaving, fists clenched. It might have been Gary's truck. It might have been one of Hydemann's. He had no way of knowing and there sure was no one he dared ask.

His stomach growled. Angel squinted up at the sun – he figured it was maybe three in the afternoon. Head down, he trudged along the gravel road and onto the shoulder of the highway. As the motel's faded sign came into view, he wondered uneasily how bad he'd catch it. If Gary was in one of his moods, Angel might be real sorry he'd left – real soon.

For a few minutes he stood there, shifting his pack around, kicking at pebbles and dust. Somewhere there must be some cactus blooming, because he could smell that smoky-sweet aroma he'd caught at Hydemann's. For a moment it distracted him with a scent so pure he could almost imagine nectar and dew on turquoise petals. And soft voices calling him...whispering his name...

A spurt of fear sharpened his breathing. Angel shook his head to clear his thoughts. Was the craziness sneaking up on him again? He started loping toward the motel rolling excuses, reasons and escape plans around in his mind. There was nothing like trying to outsmart Gary to keep a guy's wits in full thinking mode. Behind him, dust devils writhed snakelike across the pavement, stirring up a hazy, glittery cloud. If he'd looked back, he might have thought they were following him...

NINE

"Next time, at least tell me what direction you're heading." Treese passed him a slice of bread and peanut butter and mug of milky coffee. She sat on the chair opposite, chin propped up in her hand, a cup of coffee in her own favorite yellow Tweetie Bird mug steaming on the table in front of her. "My brother, Will, used to camp in the desert a lot," she said. "Him and Hydemann were friends when they were kids, y'know. More milk?"

Angel nodded and she added more milk to his mug. "Will said he thought there was some kind of old Indian magic out there," she said. "Never felt it myself."

Angel looked up at her from under his lashes. Old Indian magic... maybe that was it. Something from the old days that had saturated the land. Nothing to do with him.

"I didn't know you have a brother." Angel took a long sip.

Treese nodded. "He moved up to Seattle. Computers. He just loves computers. Sells 'em for some big store up there. Does alright, I guess."

Angel took a deep breath. "You think I could borrow his stuff? Go camping again, maybe for a couple of days?"

Treese picked at the crumbs scattered on the table. "Last night Gary came home drunk and just fell into bed. This morning he got up, swallowed some coffee, and then headed out again. He don't usually come in late and then turn around and leave early like that."

Angel knew what Treese was telling him. Gary hadn't realized that he was gone. But if his foster father had noticed, there was no telling how he'd take it.

"I could ask him," Angel said without much hope.

"Angel, you know the only reason Gary keeps you here is for help with the rooms. We can't get any workers out this far – not for what Gary's willing to pay. I can't get all the rooms done and check folks in and out at the same time."

"Yeah, I know." Angel bit down on his sandwich. He wanted to ask Treese if cleaning rooms was the only reason she would keep him. But why ask to get kicked? "If business gets slow so you don't need so much help, is it okay with you if I go up to the desert camping?" he said instead. "If I can make it okay with Gary?"

Treese stirred her coffee and shrugged. "Don't see how you could. But what's left of Will's gear is in the shed."

A crunch of tires in the parking lot sent Treese to the front desk to register the first of the night's guests. Angel spent a long time looking out the window at the desert. Somehow he had to get up into those mountains. If he had to, he'd take the gear and risk the repercussions of Gary throwing him back into the state system. But he had to find the turquoise, not just wander around up there. His mom's life depended on it.

But there was no chance to slip away the next day. Gary hung around the motel, making phone calls and scribbling notes on a flurry of scrap paper. Angel tried to get a look as he hurried by on errands for Treese, but Gary kept his arm protectively over his pages. Once he took a swat at Angel when the boy got too close, but it was half-hearted – almost good-humored for Gary. In the late morning when Angel answered the desk phone, a man identified himself as from the Arundel Mining Equipment Company. Angel handed the phone over to Gary immediately, but the call put him in a fever of anxiety. Had Gary found the vein of turquoise? *His* turquoise?

Just after lunch, John Hydemann's white convertible pulled into the parking lot. Angel spotted it over a bundle of sheets he was carrying to the laundry cart. His heart gave a thud of panic.

Angel dumped the bedding into the cart, planning to slip back out to the desert before anyone asked questions. He was just edging to the corner of the motel, when Hydemann's housekeeper, Ana, stepped out of the passenger side of the car and caught sight of him.

"There he is, Mr. Hydemann! Hello!" she waved energetically at Angel. It was too late to run, so he just stood there as dull heat crept up his neck and cheeks. Celsa slid out of the back seat and gave him a wave and smile.

Ana lifted a shoebox tied with a purple ribbon from the seat and came over to Angel. Celsa trailed her. Mr. Hydemann followed, a friendly smile on his face.

"Angel! You are an angel truly, for saving *señor* Hydemann from those snakes," Ana declared. She thrust the box toward him, managing to pat the backs of his hands as she did so. "He asked that I bake my special ginger cookies for you – a little thank you for the hero!"

Angel stood silently, gripping the box. The two adults crowded around him. He stared down at Mr. Hydemann's scuffed boots, Ana's white sandals. A few steps back, Celsa's feet were in bright pink flip-flops decorated with improbable plastic flowers. Their shoes stirred up small whirls of dust. Angel's eyes fixated on Celsa's bright pink toenail polish – it was the vibrant color of rare cactus flowers. A smile almost hovered on his lips just from that.

"You didn't give me a chance to thank you." Mr. Hydemann's hand gripped his shoulder. Angel tensed angrily and immediately dropped his eyes again. "That was pretty amazing the way you chased away those rattlers?" The man turned the statement into a question. *How?* was what he was really asking.

Angel stood stiffly, burrowing into silence. If the rancher was so grateful, why wouldn't he leave him alone? What did he want from him? Angel didn't trust the man, not at all.

The fingers on his shoulder tightened. "I'm curious about that Indian chant you used. I've only heard that once before – a long time ago," the rancher continued. His voice was light and friendly, but Angel heard a hard urgency beneath it.

What if he shook the man off, turned his back and ran into the desert? Useless. Better to play dumb. But he really wanted the rancher to get his hand off his shoulder.

"Is that something you learned from your mother, Angel?"

"I don't know," he mumbled. "Guess I heard it somewhere."

How did Mr. Hydemann know about his mother? Was the rancher checking up on him? Had he called the state hospital? Had he been asking questions about his mother? Rage flamed into Angel's stomach.

"Where did you hear it?" Hydemann demanded. Angel scowled at the ground – nothing he said would do him any good.

"Why don't you answer *señor* Hydemann?" Mrs. Reyna demanded. "Is something wrong?"

"Maybe he's scared," Celsa interrupted. "Everybody knows *señor* Hydemann doesn't want anyone in his desert."

"Celsa!" Mrs. Reyna exclaimed. She tried to put a hand over her daughter's mouth, but with an angry flick of her head, Celsa stepped back. "Isn't that true, *señor?*"

Angel risked a glance at the man towering over him. The rancher frowned. "I don't think I can get too angry this time," he said. "Not when Angel saved my life."

"So it's okay for Angel to hike in the desert? He'd be really happy if you gave him permission to say, come over and visit his friends at the ranch house," Celsa persisted. She sweetened her question with a flirtatious tilt of her head.

"Celsa!" Mrs. Reyna repeated.

"No Mama," Celsa said. "*Señor* Hydemann says he's grateful to Angel. I was wondering how grateful he is, that's all."

The rancher's eyes flashed, but then he chuckled. "I'm that grateful, Celsa." His fingers dug a little more into Angel's shoulder. "Just stay close to the road and the trail to the ranch house. The desert can be dangerous – even if you can charm snakes – and I don't want anyone hurt."

"Okay…thanks." When Angel's eyes flicked up, he saw a smug smile flash across Celsa's face.

"John!" Gary's voice pierced the air. "Hey man, it's good to see you. Can I offer you a cold one?" His gaze slid past Angel, Celsa and Ana, and dismissing them as unimportant, returned to the rancher.

Angel felt, rather than saw Mr. Hydemann stiffen. Finally, the rancher's hand dropped from his shoulder. "Thank you, no. We're on our way to town. I just wanted to thank your son here for his timely rescue the other day."

Gary's quick eyes darted to Angel then back. "Say what?"

"Didn't he tell you? Angel is quite a hero. He saved me from three rattlers."

Suspicion glinted in Gary's eyes, then he smiled, put his arm over Angel's shoulders and tousled his foster son's hair. It was all Angel could do not to jerk away.

"Naw, he didn't tell me," Gary said, "but my boy's not one for braggin'."

There was more talk, and then the ranch people climbed into the big white car. Gary stood there waving, his arm still draped on Angel's shoulders, until the rancher's car had spun out of the parking lot. Then he pulled back his arm and his cheerful look.

"I don't want you sucking up to Hydemann," Gary ordered. "I don't want him around here nosin' out my business." He started to walk away and then abruptly turned. "And what were you doin' out there by Hydemann's place anyhow?"

"Nothin," Angel answered sullenly. "I finished cleaning so I went for a walk out back." When Gary still stared, Angel scrambled for more story. "I saw a coyote, so's I was looking for its den. Mr. Hydemann scared up a rattler's nest. I helped chase 'em away, is all."

Gary snorted and kept on going. Angel threw his box of cookies into the cart, shoved it along to the next room, and returned to work.

That night Gary again took out his turquoise stones and spread them on a white towel on the kitchen table. Angel stood as close as he dared, but when Gary elbowed him away, he ended up with his back pressed against the wall. He couldn't bear to leave. The stones haunted him with memories of sun-seared landscapes and questing wind. Treese moved about the kitchen in her deliberate way, not making a fuss, but not looking either. Gary sat in front of the array of stones, silently turning them this way and that. Angel's desperate rage fanned up from his belly and he wanted to snatch the gemstones from Gary's hands. He thought he might be starting to hear the voices again…

"You want a Coke?" Treese asked. Angel plummeted back to the dim kitchen.

"No…thanks," he murmured.

"Suit yourself." She went into the office and the machine clanged.

The lamp hanging overhead wasn't very good and the stones looked a deeper blue, almost grayish in that light. Restlessly, Angel wondered if Gary's stones were the same sky blue as the turquoise he had found yesterday. If the color was different, then Gary's rock had come from another source.

Finally Angel pulled himself away and went into his bedroom. Taking the box where he stashed his few treasures from under the bed, he took out the sheared off turquoise, and slipped back into the kitchen. Gary was reaching into the fridge for a beer so Angel quickly held his rock upward in the kitchen light. Was the blue the same...or a hint different?

"Get away from there," Gary growled, swiveling around.

Frustrated, but unwilling to risk a slap, Angel faded back quickly. He returned to his room, put the stone back in his box, and flopped onto the narrow bed. Folding his arms behind his head, he stared up at the sloped, dingy ceiling. There was no way he could get close to Gary's turquoise. There was no way of knowing if he was competing for the same vein as Gary.

His fingers traced the shape of the turquoise dragon beneath his shirt. Gary was bigger, stronger and a lot meaner. But maybe, Angel thought with a cold shiver and a desperate flicker of hope, maybe Treese's brother Will had been right – maybe there was magic out here. Maybe he wasn't going crazy at all, and his talisman would help him use the desert magic.

The past few days crowded in on his mind. He saw again how Hydemann's car had hit Gary, heard the chant from the shadowy kiva, felt the dance rhythms and his surge of power when he'd ordered the snakes away from the rancher. Crazy or not, he had nothing else and Gary would do his best to keep it that way. If there really was some old Indian magic smoldering out there in the desert, he was suddenly sure the turquoise dragon given him by his father, would let him reach for it.

This had been Anasazi country. When Gary had first started talking about the mysterious pueblo tribes, Angel had looked them up on a school computer. The Anasazi had built big settlements from New Mexico west through Arizona and Colorado and north up to Utah. And then, a few hundred years ago, they'd all disappeared. Poof. Gone. Nothing left but crumbling pueblos built into cliffs and scattered rocks from their ruined kivas. No one knew where they'd gone or why or how.

Maybe it was Anasazi magic that was getting him. Or...he swallowed – Anasazi ghosts. His hand stroked the turquoise serpent lying against his chest. Was his dragon amulet some kind of ghost finder, an ancient magnet for magic? Was it dangerous? Should he get rid of it? Angel imagined taking the talisman into the desert, laying it on a sun-drenched rock and smashing it with a stone. His fingers tightened protectively over the carving. He couldn't – he just couldn't. It might give him enough power to beat Gary. Enough to save his mother. And besides, the dragon and his own sky blue eyes were all he had from his father. The carving was worth a lot – it *was* turquoise after all. Dads left their kids behind sometimes because they didn't care, but if his father had left his son something so valuable, he must have cared. Maybe he had even planned to come back.

Angel tried to imagine what his father might have looked like. Even after all his dreaming, his mental picture of his father's face was hazy... nothing ever got clear in his head but a pair of smiling blue eyes. Angel shifted restlessly. He didn't know that his Dad's eyes would smile. For all he knew, his old man's eyes might be mean and hard. But his mom had said he was nice, real nice and gentle...so Angel imagined eyes that smiled.

When he got his mom those treatments, when she got better, would she remember a little more about his father? Like his real name? Had she met him in a bar...or at a party...or out on one of the desert hikes she'd once loved? Maybe Angel would ask her when Mrs. Preston, the social worker, took him into Albuquerque tomorrow. Or if it was one of his mom's bad days, maybe not. He fell asleep thinking about it.

He is flying into the clouds, swooping over mountains and dry plains. The old ones are dying...all dying....

TEN

"Morning, Angel," Mrs. Preston said when he slid into her car the next morning. "How does this fine day find you?"

"Okay," Angel mumbled. She didn't need to know that his hands were already sweating and he was ready to throw up with nerves. Sometimes he wanted to just stop going to see his mom, but he always hoped that maybe this time she would have escaped the dust-laden winds that clouded her mind.

As soon as they turned out of the motel parking lot onto the highway, he rolled down the window and propped his chin on his arm, half leaning out into the wind. The hot air seared his skin and made him squint his eyes, but it felt good. Off in the far distance another thunderstorm was caught on the mountains, probably dropping buckets of water. The rain was a blurry grey column leaking out of a dark cloud that smudged the rest of the blue sky.

"I got a couple of doughnuts in that bag beside your seat," the social worker said. "I was waiting for you to help me eat them – sort of save me from myself, Angel." She laughed companionably and Angel felt a sliver of a smile on his lips. He liked Mrs. Preston. She was big – very big – and she laughed a lot. Her vibrantly bright clothes only half matched; the heat made big sweat circles under her arms and popped up beads of moisture on her face. But she was kind and in Angel's world that was rare.

"How long a visit we got?" he asked a few minutes later, licking the chocolate frosting from his fingers.

Mrs. Preston mopped her face with a crumpled paper napkin from the coffee shop. "We have officially an hour," she said. "But I cleared my schedule so if it's a good day for your mom, we can stay a while longer."

Angel nodded. "Good. Thanks."

He knew that probably they wouldn't need the extra time, but he was grateful that Mrs. Preston had thought of it. Just as he was always silently grateful after each depressing visit when she patted his arm and said she thought his mom might be a bit better next time.

The hospital was a massive reddish building, designed to look like an old adobe hacienda, only a lot bigger. Tourists sometimes posed outside, snapping pictures and smiling.

He and Mrs. Preston walked through the main building, all the way to the back to get to the psychiatric wing. They had to be admitted through locked doors into the sitting room that the patients used. Some of the patients gripped chair arms and watched the doors with haunted eyes. Some stared at walls and mumbled to themselves. Some of the patients simply leaned against the visitors who loved them.

Angel anxiously searched out his mom while Mrs. Preston settled herself in a chair near the door. She always spent this time either reading or talking to lonely patients.

Angel found his mom scrunched up a chair in a far corner of the long room. Her hair hung in lanky strands to her shoulders. She gazed out the window, her face set in motionless lines. Angel took a breath and slid into the chair beside her.

"Hey, Mom," he said.

His mother didn't look, didn't even appear to have heard him. Angel took one of the limp hands lying in her lap. It was pasty white – not tanned any more from the sun she'd loved.

"Hey, Mom," he repeated. "It's me, Angel. How you doin', Mom?"

He waited, hoping.

"I been thinkin'," she said, her voice so low he could hardly hear her. "I been thinkin' an' thinkin'. An' I don't know whether he eats prickly pear when he's blue or when he ain't. But they ain't blue, you know…"

Angel evened his breath and tried again. "Hey Mom, look at me. It's Angel. You remember me, don't you?"

Her eyes moved slowly from the window to his face. They widened a moment and flickered in recognition. Her hand tightened, squeezing his fingers.

"Angel," she breathed. "Hey, my Angel. You being a good boy, these days?"

"Yeah, Mom. I'm real good. You don't have to worry about me," he whispered. "How you doin'?"

Her brows puckered, making her face all puzzled. She leaned forward, still gripping his hand. "Angel," she said. "Do you eat prickly pear when you're blue?"

He lifted and dropped his shoulders a little. "I ate one the other day, out in the desert. I wasn't sad or anything."

His mother shook her head, desperation haunting her eyes. "Not when you're blue, Angel. When you're *blue!* Did you eat it when you was *blue?*" She looked at him eagerly. "You are blue sometimes, ain't you? You got them blue, blue eyes, like your Daddy..." Her eyes drifted to the window again. Her mouth drooped. *"Ladybug, ladybug..."* she sang softly to herself. Then she was silent.

Angel sat with her for the whole hour, holding her hand, trying once in awhile to talk to her, but her eyes never left the window and she didn't seem to hear him at all. When the hour was up, he let go and walked out with Mrs. Preston, not looking left or right. Just at the door, he glanced back real fast, hoping maybe his mom would care he was going. She hadn't moved.

He didn't say anything on the long ride back to the motel. Mrs. Preston chattered some about how dry it was and how there'd been thunder and lightning up on the mesa near where she lived, but no rain and my, the hot weather was about killing her.

When they pulled into the motel parking lot, Angel got out of the car, slammed the door and headed back toward the desert.

"Angel!" he heard the social worker call. He didn't care. Didn't care about her, even though she was nice. Didn't care about anything except the haunted, lost look in his mother's eyes. He leapt the fence and started to run and run and run.

Maybe this time he'd never come back.

Angel's heart pounded in time to his running feet. He wanted to cover ground, to get away, to go...anywhere so long as it was away from himself.

He ran and ran. Dust devils sprang up everywhere, choking him with whirling dust as the wind clattered and sighed across the barren landscape. Angel swerved farther and farther toward the rugged terrain he'd never explored. He tried to escape the clogging clouds of dust. He wanted to run, not gasp for breath.

Finally Angel stopped. His feet had found their way into a narrow canyon that cut back behind the Hydemann ranch house. The sides of the ravine were cracked with broken rocks and scrubby half dead plants. Pinnacles of reddish rock rose in the sky, making the landscape look like a ruined city. Angel let his breathing slowly return to normal as desert healing seeped into his heart. Could this pure desert air help his mom?

He pushed the day's picture of his mom aside, bringing back an old laughing memory instead – that was the only way he'd think of her until she was healed. Turquoise was what he needed. He walked along the bottom of the ravine, scanning the scattered rock for gleams of blue among the brilliant reds, pinks and yellows of the flowering cacti that clung to the rocky sides.

It was weird the way the steep walls of the ravine seemed to channel the breezes into a line of spinning dust. When he moved along the narrow floor, a line of haze behind him moved too. He tried to go down a promising cleft in the ravine, but the dust devils stirred up so much grit into the air that he turned back. Angel shrugged – another desert mystery he didn't understand.

Trying to ignore the pushing dust clouds, he explored slowly. The ground was ridged with upthrust rocks and pockmarked cliffs. Wind and blown dirt had scoured the rock into carved and hollowed shapes; stone slabs leaned at crazy angles. Except for the muttering wind, the silence was profound. On one slope, his foot dislodged some rock, sending it sliding and clattering down into the ravine.

A wavering cry pierced the stillness. *"Help! Ayuda! Someone... He..e..e..l..p!"*

ELEVEN

"Help me...please! " The cry had faltered in the hot air like a mirage.

"Who's there?" Angel shouted back. Maybe it was desert craziness again. He gripped his talisman. He looked back, feeling like eyes were watching him. Nothing. Just the whirls of dust devils circled behind.

"Ayuda! Please, help me!"

The cry was firmer now. Not fading in and out.

Angel ran toward the sound. He climbed a scramble of pale rock, wove past stunted pines and yellow chamisa flowers, making his way steadily toward a chimneystack of red rock. He was sure the cry had come from that direction.

At the top of the ridge he paused. "Where are you?" he shouted.

"Here! I'm here! In the ravine!"

Angel followed the voice until he found Celsa a third of the way down a slope, wedged against a weathered pinnacle with a huge stone pinning her leg against the ground. Sun beat down on her. Dried blood smeared the stones. A canteen, half-covered by loose rock, lay out of reach of her groping fingers.

"Celsa, are you okay?" Angel cried.

The girl looked up blearily, eyes dull with pain. He saw her fight to regain control of herself. She tried to smile.

*"Hay Dios...*I'm really glad to see you," she whispered through cracked lips. "I've been stuck here since this morning." She tried to smile again. "I should have known it would be you who came to rescue me. No snakes for you to charm though..."

He climbed down to her, clenching his teeth as rocks skittered from beneath his feet and plunged down the slope. The whole bank was unstable. Above him were more loose rocks – all ready to crash down on the two of them. He wouldn't think about what those small boulders could do to their flesh and bones if they came loose. Instead, he carefully watched where he put his weight, testing each footfall. His ankle twisted sharply as a rock shifted and rolled downhill, taking a small avalanche of stones with it. He teetered and then regained his balance.

"*Cuidado...*Careful...please," Celsa whispered. "The ground's been undercut from the last flood. Everything's loose."

Angel grunted and clambered the last few feet to reach her. He knelt beside Celsa, gently pushing her thick hair from her sweaty face. She forced a weak smile and he found himself smiling back. Even sunburned, bruised, and scraped, he thought she was beautiful. For a moment she gripped his hand and he could tell she was fighting back tears from pain and maybe relief.

"Can you get the rock off of me?" Her voice quavered. "I don't know how much more I can stand."

"Don't worry. I'll get you out." Angel squeezed her fingers, and with a knot in the pit of his stomach, studied the boulder that pinned her down. The stone probably weighed a couple of hundred pounds or more. How could he move it? But he had to.

"Can you hand me my canteen?" Celsa asked. "I...I've been hallucinating. Seeing big snake things...I need some water bad."

Angel pulled the canteen from the rocks and unscrewed the lid, steadying her hand as she held it to her lips. She drained it in obvious relief, and then leaned back with her eyes shut. Angel squatted by her again. "Do you think your leg's broken?"

She shook her head slightly. "It's not broken. There's a smaller rock underneath that kept the big one from smashing my leg."

"The rock is really big – I don't know if I can move it by myself, and if I dropped it, you could get hurt a lot worse," he told her. "I'll have to go to the ranch for help. Can you hang on a while longer?

She paused, seeming to force herself to breath evenly. "There's no one at the ranch house. *Mi mam*á and sister and all the women and kids went to visit my Aunt Junie – she had twins last week...and then one of the men drove in – yelled that a flash flood had stranded one of the herds in Cholla Canyon. *Mi papá* and brothers and all the men headed out. I didn't want to go to my aunt's, so *Mi mam*á told me to stay at the ranch house."

Angel sucked in his breath. It was miles to another ranch. Gary was probably gone and what could Treese do that Angel couldn't? It would take him at least an hour to get to the motel anyway. Even if Treese telephoned for help it might take awhile for an ambulance to get to them, and the way down here was so rough and steep, the paramedics would only be able to bring the vehicles part way. It might take hours for help to get to Celsa.

He licked his dry lips, glanced up at the burning sun, and then back at the girl. Her face was pale around the lips and she was breathing in short, shallow pants. Shock and heat were overwhelming her defenses. Angel realized with a rush of panic that Celsa wouldn't last out here much longer. He'd have to try himself. Somehow, he had to save her.

He felt around the edges of the boulder, checking to see where it was wedged against the other rock and where it pressed against Celsa's leg. She said nothing, just lay unmoving with clenched teeth. It must hurt like crazy, Angel thought. She was a lot braver than he thought he would be.

Gripping his hands around the rock sides, he gave an experimental pull. Nothing. Angel took off his hat and wiped his brow.

"If you're not using your hat, I wouldn't mind getting this sun off my face," Celsa whispered.

Angel handed it to her and she settled it over her face.

"I'm going to look for a lever to push with," he told her. "Just holler if you're worried about anything. I'm not leaving you."

It took him ages to find a branch large enough, and even then it was so dry he didn't think it would bear the rock's weight. There seemed to be dust devils skittering everywhere and they were making him crazy with their flying grit, dirt and clattering pebbles.

He hauled the branch back to Celsa. She had the hat tipped way over her eyes and seemed to be resting. Angel squatted beside her again.

"I found a branch," he said. "But I don't know if it'll work. It's real dry."

Celsa pushed back the hat and looked at him, almost uncomprehending. "You've got to try something," she whispered. "I don't...I don't think I can last much longer."

She didn't look good at all. Her lips were now bluish and her face had a sheen of sweat that didn't look healthy. He shaded her as much as he could with his body, but with the heat radiating from the rocks, it didn't do any good.

"Will you be able to move quick, if I can shift the rock?" he asked.

She hesitated, seemed to force herself together, and then nodded. "I can do it."

Angel gave her hand another squeeze and then got started. Picking out a good sized rock, he lugged it over to make a fulcrum for the wooden branch. He shoved the tip of the branch under the rock's edge, and was about to push, when he paused. With one hand he pulled out his turquoise serpent. Gripping it tightly, he shut his eyes.

If ever there was a time for desert magic…

"Grandfather, help me," he whispered.

The whirring in the background got louder; the dragon pulsed under his fingers. Letting go, he threw all his strength into forcing down the lever. The branch bent…the rock was moving! Shifting…grinding… Celsa gasped and locked her hands under her knee, ready to jerk free.

Crack! The branch snapped.

Celsa screamed. Angel threw himself forward, grabbed the rock and heaved. His body arched up and backward, willing, shoving the boulder away. The girl rolled out from under its shadow. With a gasp, Angel let go. The rock crashed to the ground, splintering stones, sending rocks bounding down the slope.

Chests heaving, they didn't move for several minutes. Celsa lay sideways, one arm still locked under her leg. With her other hand she scrubbed her eyes. Her shoulders shook.

"You okay?" Angel kneeled beside her, slipping his arm beneath her shoulders to support her.

She lifted her face toward him and forced a smile. "Yeah. I am. *Gracias.*"

For a moment he held her, feeling the soft contours of her shoulders against him. Then stiffly, slowly, she uncurled her body, and got to her feet. Angel grabbed her arm to steady her.

"I'm okay," she said huskily. "Nothing broken. I'm good. *Muy bien.*"

She closed her eyes briefly, and then with shaking fingers, examined two big tears in her jeans. The material was crusted in dried blood and dirt. As she pulled back the fabric, Angel saw her flesh was purple and brown with grit ground into a deep, ugly gash.

"That looks bad," he said.

"It hurts like…well, you know. But it'll heal," she said and forced another smile. "I'm not dead…" She paused and swallowed. "…and… and if I can get back fast enough, no one will ever know I left the house."

Angel frowned and watched as Celsa took several deep breaths, obviously gathering the few reserves of strength she had left. "Why'd you come out here anyway?"

She busied herself smoothing back the torn fabric and didn't meet his eyes. "I had something to do…" She stared owlishly at the blood-smeared rock, and then back at Angel. "How did you lift it? When the branch cracked, I thought I was dead! How did you hold up that rock?"

Angel shrugged and grinned, feeling a flush of embarrassment rising in his face. With mock heroics he flexed his arms. They were still thin even though he could feel the hot blood swelling his muscles. "Muscle man…" he tried to joke, then shrugged. "I just grabbed it. I guess it wasn't as heavy as I thought."

Celsa tilted her head sideways as she continued to stare it him. "No, it was that heavy. I've heard about people getting an adrenaline rush," she said slowly, "and doing *loco* things like picking up a car to save a kid in an emergency. But that isn't what's weird. You turned blue. I mean there was this blazing blue light all around you. And senor Hydemann said you had a blue…a blue aura when you sang to those snakes."

"That's just stupid," Angel snapped. "No, I didn't!"

"*Si*, you did," Celsa's voice was absolutely certain. "I saw it."

"You've been out in the sun all day," Angel fought back a surge of panic. His mother had asked him if he was turning blue. "If you aren't hallucinating, you're just crazy!"

Celsa blinked a couple of times and with a long, ragged breath, leaned against a column of rock for support. "Whatever. I have to go home." She turned and laboriously started the harsh climb up the bank.

Angel watched her, torn. He wanted to run…to get away from her stupid ideas. And he wanted to help her, keep being a hero somehow.

She stumbled and he leapt forward to grab her.

"You can't hike two miles back to the ranch with your leg like that." He scowled, determined to get her home. He tried taking her arm, but she shook him off.

"I'm fine," she snapped.

Fuming, Angel stomped along about five feet back of her. The wind had dropped a little and the dust devils had whirled away, so the air was easy to breathe again. Celsa limped slowly but steadily. Reluctantly, he admired her courage, again. And her stubbornness. They didn't say a word to each other right up to the smoothed edge of the ranch house grounds.

Nothing moved but the old white dog sleeping in the shade of an out building, his paws twitching as he chased some phantom jack rabbit. Celsa limped slowly toward one of the neat cottages set between the barns and main house. Angel followed, ready to grab her if she collapsed. Her stumbling walk was getting slower and slower. The glimpses of her face showed it white with her lip clenched between her teeth. She's tough, Angel thought.

Opening the screened door, she turned. "*Gracias*," she managed.

"I'm coming in," he said. "You're going to need help cleaning and bandaging your leg."

"No..." she started.

"Unless you want to ask your mom to do it when she gets back," he shoved his hands in his pockets and waited. When he was maybe eight or nine, his mother had taught him first aid. She'd said if they were hiking and got hurt, they had both better know what to do.

"Oh, all right," Celsa grunted.

Angel followed her inside and sat on a worn kitchen chair while she went into a bedroom to peel off her jeans. The room was small with a big sofa on one wall, a TV against another, and the kitchen taking up one end of the room. A large loom with a half finished piece of cloth took up the wall near the window. He thought the place looked homey and very clean although the table, chairs and counter were worn. Celsa's mom had gone to a lot of trouble to make it pretty. Bright patterned curtains fluttered on the window, crocheted lace lay on the back and arms of the sofa, and a vase held a bouquet of bright, sweet-smelling flowers

When Celsa limped out, wearing loose shorts, Angel caught his breath. Where her skin wasn't gashed open, it was covered in dried blood. Along her thigh, just above her knee, Celsa's leg looked like a chunk of meat from the butcher. It oozed purplish blood.

Angel swallowed. He didn't know how she was still walking. "You ought to get your mom to take you to the doctor," he said.

"She can't afford the doctor, not even for a copay," Celsa said harshly. "My sister, Jenny, is going to community college in the fall. No one in our family ever went to college before and I'm not using her money because I was stupid."

"You need to see a doctor," Angel argued.

"Well, I won't," Celsa supported herself by leaning heavily on a table. "If you can't help, then go home and I'll look after this myself."

"Like you won't about die while you do it." Angel snorted.

"Like I won't even blink." Her dark eyes stormed like thunderheads.

They glared at each other. Angel shrugged and a smile tugged at his mouth. "You got a first aid kit?"

Celsa waited a beat then nodded. "In the bathroom. In a plastic box under the sink."

Angel got the box and a couple of towels. Kneeling in front of Celsa's leg, he looked at it closely. "It's gonna hurt when I clean it. You'd better sit on the floor."

She said nothing but levered herself down onto the tile. He scrubbed his hands at the sink, and then folded the towels into a pad under her leg. The skin had been torn and crumpled so her muscle showed underneath. He could even see a bluish vein that had been nicked. If that had been sliced open....

"I need a cup," he said.

Celsa pointed to a cupboard.

Angel chose a measuring cup and then took a bottle of hydrogen peroxide from the box. Remembering what his mother had taught him, he mixed the peroxide with some cool water, then slowly poured the mixture over the wound. Celsa gasped and gave a little moan. The mixture foamed inside the gash, bubbling out grit and grime. Ignoring Celsa's sharp intakes of breath, Angel kept pouring until the liquid ran clear and most of the dirt had washed onto the towel.

"I've got to clean it some more," he said. "It'll hurt a lot."

"Hurry up, then," Celsa whispered.

Angel put more water on a clean gauze pad and as gently as he could, wiped the last of the dirt and old blood from the wound. Then he poured some clean water over it.

"You'd be better having a doctor fix this," he said as he patted it dry. "It's going to leave a bad scar."

Celsa shrugged. "I don't care. Do you...do you have to stitch it?"

"I can't," Angel said, recoiling at the idea. "I don't have the stuff, and I don't know how. But I'll get it straight for healing."

"Good...thanks."

Being as careful as he could, Angel pulled out the bruised, folded-back skin and smoothed it over the wound. He pressed it gently with his thumbs until it seemed to stick. As he got bandages out of the box he glanced at his friend. Her eyes were glassy and her face was dull white, but she was still gripping her lip with her teeth and staring determinedly at a painting of Jesus on the wall.

Angel smeared an antibiotic ointment on another gauze pad and pressed it against the wound. He used adhesive tape to stick it in place.

"That's it," he said, sitting back on his heels.

Celsa slowly stood up. "I'm going to bed," she whispered. "I still feel really sick."

"You want me to stay until your family gets back?"

She shook her head. "No. There'd be too many questions."

He waited in the living room until he heard the creak of bed-springs, the whuff of blankets being pulled up, then a soft sigh. Angel let himself out. As he crossed the smooth turf heading toward the desert, a roaring cloud of dust bounced from the untamed lands onto the ranch drive. With a squeal, the white truck pulled up. John Hydemann, splattered from head to foot with dried mud, stepped out and looked Angel up and down.

"We meet again, Angel," he said.

TWELVE

Angel kept his gaze turned down. He didn't want the rancher looking at his eyes again, asking about how come they were such a weird color. "I came to see Celsa," he muttered finally. "I'm late. I gotta go home."

Forgetting that Hydemann "owned" it, Angel turned toward the desert again. He wanted to be out there, to lose himself in its peaceful beauty. The day had been too long and too hard.

"Wait a minute," the rancher said. He sprinted the few feet between them and put his hand on Angel's shoulder.

"Leave me alone!" Angel yelled. He twisted away and ran full out into the desert. He heard the rancher shouting behind him, but he kept on going, letting the hot wind carry the words away.

Coming at last to his special place, he crawled into the small cave formed by the leaning stones. He really felt like a desert animal now – one that wanted to hide in a dark burrow. This place was more his home than the cramped room at the motel. For long moments he rested in the cool silence, then taking one of the water bottles, eased himself back out. He downed the liquid, and then rubbed his arm across his mouth and sat, leaning against the stones, letting twilight wash over him.

The open sky was streaked with glowing gold that paled to rose and purple as sunset approached. The scents of cactus flowers and animal musk played in his nostrils. Soft whispers and crackled foot falls drifted into his ears. Every sense grew and sharpened until he seemed to "see" with his nose, his tongue, his ears and his skin. He became one with the desert.

"The eagles are my brothers..." he whispered. His shoulders swayed in the memory of powerful wing thrusts. *His heart soared upward. He wheeled and turned in the gusting wind, circling his home above the dry mountains.*

"I am greater than the eagles..."

A boy, almost a man, trots doggedly along the trail. At his belt, a flute thumps against his hip. In his arms he carries a gift...a burden... Angel whirls downward to the land, to the boy...he is the boy.

Once again Angel travels the straight road to his kiva. The memory unfolds, as though it has always been there, waiting...

Memories of a coughing sickness that singing does not cure. Memories of stunted crops yellowing in the parched ground. Memories of empty-bellied enemies creeping upon them in the night...

The elders say the spirits are angry. They say the spirits have gone away to their homes in the sacred mountain and will no longer dance against evil with the people. It is all because the young men spit on the ground at their whirling feet. The spirits do not forgive and the people are dying.

In the kiva, the children cry in hunger and the fathers and mothers cry in fear. Thunderbird screams in the mountains but he does not bring rain. Everything is dying.

The grandfather stands. The people quiet in hope.

"We once were one family with Tieholtsodi, the water serpent of the third world," he says. "We must go to her and beg her to save us."

The people are joyful now. They have heard the story of coyote and Tieholtsodi's stolen children all their lives.

"But where is the hole in the world?" the grandson asks.

"It is remembered," the grandfather says. "You will go to Tieholtsodi and plead for us. But you must be swift, for I see our death on the horizon."

"I will go," the young man says. "I will be swift."

At dawn the people walk in a long column toward the sacred mountain. As they go, they sing the songs of remembering. The boy and the grandfather walk at the head of the column. Their enemies watch but do not attack. They too, know the power of the songs and will not anger the spirits further by killing the singers.

The people pace between the two guardian rocks, along an empty ravine to the cave of Tieholtsodi.

"Come to the house of Tieholtsodi," the grandfather sings.

"We come to her house," the people chant.

"We come to the house of our clan mother," the grandfather sings.

"We come to the fire of our clan," the people reply.

SUSAN BROWN   71

In the turquoise cave, the boy endures the ceremony of cleansing. Purified in body and spirit, he travels deeper into the sacred mountain. It was all as his grandfather described. Through the tunnel where Tieholtsodi's breath roars in his ears, past the towering columns of turquoise where the life of the people has been carved, to the dark pool where, between the carved claws of Tieholtsodi, he finds the magic reed. Taking a great breath, he dives down, and then pulls himself hand over hand, deeper and deeper. The icy water drives feeling from his slipping hands. He is sure he will die. His lungs burst and he gasps. But instead of water, he gulps air. The sweet air of the fourth world!

He stands on the sacred mountaintop of that world. It is very beautiful but empty since all the people and animals had fled upward to the fifth world. In that empty place, he sings a song of his loneliness.

I stand alone
I sing alone
My heart is lost to me
My heart travels...

Once again he finds the hole in the world. Once again he plunges downward until he reaches the third world. It too is beautiful and empty – almost.

Tieholtsodi, the feathered serpent lives here with her children.

He walks for four days until on the evening of the fourth day he comes to the great lake where the mother of serpents lives.

"Tieholtsodi!" he cries. "I have come!"

The great dragon surges from the water, coiling into the sky. Her wings beat the air and a gale rages across the land. The boy leans into the wind and waits.

Tieholtsodi roars and landslides wrack the mountains. The boy spreads his feet on the rolling earth and waits.

Tieholtsodi screams and lightning shatters the sky. The boy opens his arms to the flashing night and waits.

Tieholtsodi's tail thrashes and the clouds split open. The boy raises his face to the rain and plays his flute – a prayer of memory and entreaty.

Tieholtsodi regards him with her glittering turquoise eyes. Water glistens on the two horns that crown her narrow head. She folds her feathered gold and red tipped wings against her back.

"Who has come?" she demands. "Who calls me?"

"I have called you, Tieholtsodi. I am a son of your clan. We need your help, old mother." The boy tells her about the hunger, sickness and desperate enemies. He begs for her strength.

She leans forward and her hot breath sears his cheek. "Come," she hisses. He climbs on her back and she flies through the clouds and sky for four days and four nights. Then she circles and settles on a great rock overlooking a basin of golden land.

"I show you my children," Tieholtsodi says. Before him romps and sleeps and rambles, many snakes and many serpents. They are all colors and all sizes. They slither, coil, fly and scamper. "My strength is in my children. If any will choose to go with you, then my strength will once again join your people."

The boy climbs down and stands among the snakes and serpents. They slither, slide and bask in the sun. All are beautiful, but one is more beautiful than all others. Her skin shines with the color of the sky that stretches open and free above his home. Once again, he plays his flute. When she turns her face to him, he holds out his arms and she takes the form of a beautiful maiden. Her hair is black as night, but shines with the light of stars. Her eyes are the color of the sky. He loves her at once and she returns that love.

In his joy, he forgets the needs of the people. He spends long days walking with Tieholtsodi's daughter in the cool meadows of the third world. But at last, when a year has passed he remembers the people waiting for him. With Tieholtsodi's blessing her daughter makes herself into an egg so that the young man can carry her back to the fifth world. Some of Tieholtsodi's other children are jealous and so they hiss and spit. They slide into the young man's clothing, and their anger makes their spit poisonous. But he is protected by Tieholtsodi's daughter and does not feel their bites and scratches.

He climbs the magic reeds into the fourth and fifth worlds. He runs without resting through the tunnel filled with Tieholtsodi's breath, between the columns of turquoise, along the narrow ravine into the hot, open desert. He sees no one, and cries out in fear. The serpent girl's jealous sisters and brothers slither onto the land and their venom makes them dumb. Embarrassed and angry, they crawl and scamper into cracks and crevices. They live there still.

Angel runs with the young man carrying the dragon egg. He feels *the magic, feels it glowing alive and full of promise! All will be well! His people will be safe!*

He runs and runs. But the lookouts do not call to him...

There is silence. Too much silence. He is too late...

The yip of a coyote shot Angel awake. His movement startled a jack rabbit that froze, watching him with frightened eyes. Angel scrubbed his face with his arm. He still felt that hole inside him, burrowed there by the memories of the other boy who had also lost his family. It gnawed him from the inside, so that his belly felt hollow and bleeding – but Angel knew nothing showed on the outside. There was nothing to show such loss and grief but pouchy, dark circles under haunted eyes. He thought of his mom's eyes then, of the eyes of all the people in her hospital. He wished that he could do something, anything to heal them. No one in the world deserved to hurt that much. No one.

He gripped his talisman then, and shut his eyes. He was distantly aware that animals were creeping closer and closer, sitting in a ring like the shadowy people of the kiva.

His heart was bursting with longing and compassion for all the people's pain, for his own loneliness. He held the talisman in both hands and began to sing the boy's song, softly then more and more surely…as he remembered.

I stand alone
I sing alone
My heart is lost to me
My heart travels
Travels the shadow path
The path my people walk.
Come back to me my people
Come back to the time of dreams and laughter
Come back before I am lost on the shadow paths.
I cannot walk without you
I cannot sing without you
I am afraid of the shadow path
That does not bear your footprints.
I call you back to me
I sing you back to me

My heart cries for your heart
Do not leave me to walk
The shadow path alone.

The night was still. In the distance Angel heard soft singing… chants that called to him, echoing his own voice. He opened his eyes and stood up in the velvet night. Above him the moon and stars pierced the black sky the way his grief pierced his breath. He held up his arms to the sweeping night, facing the western mountain – the sacred mountain. The eyes of the desert creatures shone yellow in the silent moonlight. He felt their hearts beating fast and slow, counterpoint and echo to his own desperate longing.

Above, wingbeats thrummed slowly in the air. They were coming… he knew they were coming!

"I'm here!" he cried. "I'm here!"

A harsh white light blazed over the landscape. With skitters of terror, the animals bolted into the night. The wingbeats faded and were gone.

"No!" Angel cried.

The light swept across his face, blinding him. "What in the name of all git out are you doin'" Gary demanded. His hand caught Angel hard on the cheek, sending him sprawling.

THIRTEEN

Angel lay on the ground blinking into the flashlight held by his foster father.

"I found him!" the man shouted over his shoulder.

Treese, wearing a loose jacket and a worried expression ran up and crouched over Angel. "You hurt, Angel?" she demanded. Her fingers searched out his forehead.

"I'm fine," Angel thrust her hand away and sat up, glaring at Gary.

"You stupid, little piece of dog…"Gary raged.

"That's enough," Treese said sharply. "He's been out in the desert for hours and he's hurt."

"Not as hurt as he ought to be," Gary grumbled. "That old bag social worker is threatening to call the cops if we don't find you, ya little…"

"Lay off, Gary," Treese's voice held more steel than Angel remembered hearing before.

Gary sullenly played the light over Angel's hideout, then crouched to root around in the cache.

"Leave my stuff alone!" Angel cried.

"Your stuff," Gary snorted. "That's rich. Seems to me these here blankets at one time were the property of the Lone Butte Motel. Correct me if I'm wrong, Angel, but when you take somethin' that ain't yours, some people call it stealing!"

Angel said nothing. What could he say?

"C'mon, Gary," Treese said. "Let's get on home."

"No…no…" Gary snapped. "I just want to take a look at what other personal property our little Angel has acquired. Now, what have we here?"

He tugged out the worn bandana. Angel tore himself from Treese and tried to grab it. "Leave that!" he yelled. "That's mine!"

Gary shoved him away and ripped the worn fabric. He played his light on the blue stones that cascaded into his hand.

"They're mine!" Angel panted. "I found, 'em Gary. I found 'em in the desert. They're going to buy treatments for my mom."

"You found 'em alright," Gary snarled. "You found 'em in my safe. You dirty little thief!" His arm swung back. Treese stepped in front of Angel. The blow hit her shoulder, making her stagger a little.

"You let him be," she hissed, rubbing her shoulder. "You touch him, Gary Tanner, and I'll make you sorry you was ever born."

"I'll tell you what I'm sorry!" he shouted. "I'm sorry I ever married a stupid cow like you!" He turned on Angel. "And you! You steal from me again and I'll break every bone in your worthless body!"

He shoved the stones in his pocket and strode off, taking the light with him.

Angel felt the tears slipping down his cheeks. He couldn't help it. Treese put her arm around his shoulder. "Don't mind him," she told Angel. "He don't mean half what he says."

"He took my turquoise, Treese," Angel whispered. "It took me weeks and weeks to find it. It was for my mom. I didn't steal it."

"C'mon," Treese sighed. "Let's go home."

They picked their way through the desert by moonlight. To Angel's eyes the land was near as bright as day. He didn't want to go back to the motel. He didn't ever want to see Gary again.

His turquoise was gone.

The phone shrilled as they walked in the back door of the motel. Gary picked it up and put on his good guy voice.

"Yeah, we found him, Mrs. Preston," he was saying. "Seems fine – just a bit upset y'know from seein' his mom so bad off. You want to say hi to him, before he goes off to bed?" Pause. "Yeah, here he is."

Gary scowled warningly at Angel as he handed him the phone. Angel took the receiver and sank onto a kitchen chair.

"Hi Angel," Mrs. Preston said. *"Are you alright?"*

"Yeah, I'm fine," he said.

"What happened, kiddo?" she asked.

Angel glanced up at Gary. His foster father managed to glare at him again as he took a beer out of the fridge.

"I just went walking in the desert," he mumbled.

"All that time?" she said. *"Do you have any idea how worried we all were?"*

"Yeah, I'm real sorry," Angel said. "I met up with a kid from school and…and I didn't realize how late it was. Then…" Glancing at Gary's face as the man popped his bottle top, he thought fast. "Then it got really dark really fast and I wasn't sure where the motel was…so I just waited where I was. You know…stay put when you get lost."

Angel felt sick at the endless lies, but Gary's face had lost the furious look. Things would settle down now.

"Well, I'm not going to pretend I'm happy about this," Mrs. Preston said. *"I'm going to drop by again in a couple of days, soon as I can clear off my schedule a bit, and we're going to talk. We'll see what we can do to help you out, Angel. That sound okay to you?"*

"That sounds fine, Mrs. Preston," Angel said. "Thanks for everything."

"Uh huh," she said. *"You go on to bed. You must be beat. Night, Angel."*

"Good night," Angel replied. He hung up the phone and when Gary's eyes were busy checking out the TV listing, he slipped into his own room. Stripping down, Angel crawled into bed. Too restless to sleep, he ran his fingers across the bone dry sheets making jabs of lightning from the static electricity. A few minutes later, Treese knocked lightly then came in with a peanut butter sandwich and a Coke.

Angel sat up gratefully. She brushed back his hair with the tips of her fingers, handed him the can, set the plate on the hollow spot between his feet and left. The sandwich was about half of what he could eat, Angel realized, as he gulped and swallowed. The clock said 10:46 as he pulled the covers back up around his shoulders. Only about seven hours before he could get some breakfast. Only seven hours until he had to look at Gary's ugly face again.

The next morning, his foster father was up early again, figuring on scraps of paper, talking and whistling softly to himself. Angel kept a wary eye on Gary, but as usual, the man had left yesterday behind and was plowing forward with his great plans for the future.

Morosely, Angel ate some toast and went to work cleaning rooms. That was about all he had to look forward to, he thought. The loss of his turquoise burned in him but he didn't know what to do. No one would believe him. And his mom would keep staring out the window with those sad, empty eyes, forever.

Angel slammed the cart into the stucco wall and just stood there, chest heaving. He had to do something. He had to. But he didn't know what.

Treese stepped out of the motel office. "Angel," she called. "Can you take some extra towels to number 12?"

Angel smacked his fist against the cart. Then he took the clean towels to number 12.

That day drifted away and another and another took its place. Angel didn't go back into the desert, didn't plan where he could find more turquoise. What was the use when Gary was just going to take it? The more gleeful Gary acted as he schemed to get rich, the more angry and hopeless Angel felt. Somewhere underneath that lay a snarl of rage burning in Angel's belly.

The third afternoon, Gary went out. With the rooms all cleaned, Angel parked on the sofa beside Treese to watch a talk show about messed up marriages. A guy had just broken down crying when Celsa walked into the office. She wore a long breezy skirt instead of jeans or shorts.

Celsa leaned on the counter. "Hi Angel. *Qué pasa?*" she said. "You doing anything?"

"Watchin' TV," he said. Duh.

Treese gave him a little push. "Why don't you get a soft drink for your friend," she said. "Get the money from the drawer."

It seemed hard to meet Celsa's eyes, so Angel busied himself getting the change from the till. "You want one, Treese?"

"Don't mind if I do," she said smiling at them both. "Angel, I can look after things here if you want to go spend time with your friend. Just be back by dinner."

"Yeah, sure," Angel said, shooting a glare in her direction. She grinned more widely and popped the top on her can of Coke.

He followed Celsa outdoors and the two of them sat on the steps in front of the motel. He felt her nearness like a warm breeze, and was hazily aware of the scent of her hair as the breeze ruffled through it.

"How's your leg?" Angel asked.

Celsa grimaced. "Kind of a mess, but it's healing and it isn't infected. You did a good job. Thanks."

Silence fell between them. Celsa swished the pop around in the can, looking at it like it was the most interesting thing in the universe.

"So, did you get in trouble?" Angel asked finally.

She shook her head. "Nobody noticed, though the King wanted to know if we spend a lot of time together. In fact, he wanted to know all about you. He was really nosey. Did you get in trouble?"

Angel took a deep, slow breath. "No. They don't care much."

She shot him a frowning look. "Your mom seems nice."

"That ain't my mom."

Celsa took a drink. "Well, she seems nice."

"She's not bad." Angel felt himself relaxing a bit.

Silence.

"Angel," Celsa said at last. "Can I tell you a secret?"

He shrugged. "I don't care."

Celsa kept going. "My family's worked on Hydemann's ranch for ages. More than ten years. And he pays good for the work, but even then it isn't much." She twisted to look him straight in the eye. "My dad and brothers and mom and sister, they work and work and save every nickel. But there's a lot of us, and uncle Ramos has a bad leg so he can't work much and Auntie Junie just had twins! And there's Jenny's college tuition."

She scowled, picked up a stone and threw it across the gravel lot as though skipping it across a lake. "I have to do something or *mi papá* will never have his auto detailing business and there won't be anything left to pay for me to go to college – and I'm going to go. I'm the smartest girl in my class and *I – am – going – to – go – to – college!*"

"Great." Angel said. "Go to college." She obviously couldn't wait to leave and he would be left alone again. The realization felt like he'd been caught in one of the flash floods that swept through the arroyos.

Celsa scowled at him. "I have a business proposition. A way to make a lot of money. Are you interested?"

Angel narrowed his eyes. She was crazy, he decided. "Maybe."

"*Bien.* You ever heard of the Anasazi?" Celsa demanded.

"Yeah. I heard of them," Angel said.

"Trying to find out what happened to them is a big deal in archeology. Aside from the turquoise…"

Now, Angel swiveled to stare at the girl.

"They traded with the Aztecs, you know. Gold, turquoise…and things that history doesn't know about," Celsa said quietly. Her hands smoothed the light fabric of her skirt over her legs. "There are ruins in the desert, Angel. One of the ranch hands went out there last year. He got drunk and went joy riding in a truck – about thirty miles in. Mr. Hydemann fired him right off, but Hector told *mi papá* about it before he left. A real city, he said, built up against the cliffs in one of the canyons."

"If he was drunk," Angel said, "maybe he imagined it?"

Celsa shrugged. "Maybe. But I think it's a lot more than that. Nobody is allowed out there. Ever. Mr. Hydemann never lets archeologists check it out and his Daddy and Granddaddy didn't either. If you and I found those ruins and took pictures, we'd be famous. And if we were famous, they'd pay us money to talk to us. Maybe give us scholarships." She looked at him sideways. "We might be able to sell some of the artifacts we find, too – maybe gold and turquoise for sure."

Angel's smile wasn't much more than a slit. Someone else who wanted to take something from Hydemann land. "You really think Mr. Hydemann is just going to let you walk off with his stuff? You think he doesn't know what's on his own land?"

Celsa dropped her head into her hands in frustration. "I don't know what he knows. I only know that my family keeps working and working and getting poorer and poorer. *No esta bien.* If I don't help them, who else will? Do you have any family? Do you know what it's like to watch people you love just lose and lose?"

"Yeah, I got an idea."

Angel stood up, dropped his can on the gravel and smashed it with his foot. Then he strode across the parking lot, away from Celsa and the motel office, until he stood in front of the fence that separated the motel from the miles and miles of Hydemann land. Was it wrong to take from someone who had so much?

Angel remembered taking a package of Juicy Fruit gum from a store when he was little, before his mom got sick. He'd loved the bright yellow and red package. But his mama hadn't gone along with it. After she had made him take it back and say he was sorry, she had taken Angel's face gently between her rough hands. "We ain't much, Angel," she'd said. "But we ain't thieves. You remember that, okay?"

He remembered. He was remembering so hard, he didn't turn when he heard Celsa limp up behind him. She stood waiting silently until he faced her.

"If we find stuff and take it, it's stealing," Angel said.

Her eyes didn't waver. "I know."

The sun was glinting now over the sacred mountain, sending rivers of gold streaming along the slopes, pooling over the undulating desert. Angel felt the warmth on his skin, smelled the scent of dust and cactus flowers flowing on the desert wind. Anger surged over him. He'd worked for turquoise – *pickin's for losers*, Gary called it – and Gary had stolen it anyway. Hidden out there in the desert was more turquoise, and why should men like King Hydemann and Gary have it all? While Angel stood around worrying if it was right or wrong, his mom looked out barred windows and smelled the odors of antiseptics and frightened people.

"Okay. I'm in."

"All right," Celsa stuck out her hand. "Partners."

Angel looked down at her hand and stopped himself from grasping it. "Why? Why do you want partners?"

"Because I can't do it myself," she said, frustration clear in her voice. "You saw what's happened to me in the desert. I've read every book the library has about survival; I've searched every website, but I can't make it work. I want to help my family – not die. You obviously know the desert."

Angel smiled, his heart suddenly lightening. She was right. He *did* know the desert. It was in his bones and blood. It was his home.

"Okay," he said. "Fifty-fifty?"

"Absolutely." Celsa's smile washed over him and he felt like stealing or not, the world was going to get a lot better.

She stood up on her toes and kissed his cheek. "Partners" she said, mischief putting sun sparks in her eyes.

When he stiffened in embarrassment, she smiled smugly, took his arm and walked him behind the back of the motel, along the edge of the desert. The touch of her hand and the casual brushing of her hips against his, made him want to run with crazy joy, except he didn't want her hand to leave his arm any time soon.

"So, here's the plan I've worked out, Angel," she said, becoming serious again. "We'll head up toward the high country, away from the herds. I don't know exactly where Hector saw the ruins but there's a whole area of the ranch back that way that Mr. Hydemann never grazes and never lets anyone go to."

"But the ranch is huge, miles and miles – how did you find that out?"

Celsa grinned. "Us housekeepers see a lot of things. In his study he's got this big map of the ranch on his wall. I've been checking it out when I'm supposed to be dusting. It's got pins for the cattle herds and buildings. Everything is really carefully marked – except for one huge section." She pointed west, toward the sacred mountain. "*Haya.* Over there," she said softly. "No one is ever allowed to go over there."

Angel's heart beat painfully in his chest. He turned and stared at the smoky blue mountain, his sacred mountain. It called him...the turquoise...the treasure... the shadow people...everything was there. No more waiting. He was going to claim it.

He glanced down at Celsa just as she looked up at him, her smile warming him like the sun. She took his hand in her own. "Partner, we're going to do it!"

FOURTEEN

It was amazing to Angel how quickly they made their plans. Celsa was the most organized person he'd ever met. While they tramped the three miles back to the Turquoise Hill Ranch and Hydemann's map, she outlined what she'd done so far.

"All the men are over in the canyons that way." Celsa gestured toward the snaggle-toothed hills that lay southwest on the open horizon. Thunderclouds still stacked up against the mountain faces.

"The flooding up there is terrible. *Señor* Hydemann's already lost six heifers," Celsa told him. "That's why we can't waste any time. I listened to the weather warnings and there are more storms coming. So far they aren't over where we're going, but who knows how long that will last."

Angel remembered his dream about the Thunderbird screaming above the mountains and a shiver of fear chilled him. Last year two people had been killed when a wall of water surged over their car. The sky had been blue where they had stalled in a ravine, but the storms in the mountains funneled the raging floods into the lowlands. The water sluiced on into the next town, sending three feet of muddy water down the main street. When the desert got water, it didn't know what to do with it.

"I've been stocking up on camp food and beef jerky," Celsa went on. "And I have my survival guides, an archeology reference book and a new first aid kit. Do you like Life Savers or Jolly Ranchers best?"

"What?"

"Hard candy is a good thing to carry," she explained. "In an emergency, for shock. I'm going to get some tonight when *mi mamá* does the shopping for the week. What do you like best?"

"I don't know…grape?" Angel replied. He grinned when Celsa rolled her eyes.

They approached the ranch house from the desert. Once again, there wasn't much activity. The white dog still dozed in the shade. A Spanish radio announcer's voice puffed out on the hot breeze.

"Hi *Mamá*!" Celsa called. She waited a moment, and when there was no response motioned for Angel to follow her. "Good. The men are out working and *Mamá* will be too busy to hear us."

They went around the house, passing first a large patio lined with pots of blooming plants and then circling a glittering swimming pool. It would sure be nice, Angel thought, to be able to dive into that cool water on these roasting days. But Celsa never paused until they reached a door at the back of the house. She pulled it open and went in. Angel followed.

It led to a small hallway with a crammed pantry on one side and the kitchen on the other. The kitchen was the most beautiful one Angel had ever seen, and almost as big as the whole living quarters at the motel. Gleaming pans hung from metal racks above the granite-topped work areas. A soft hum rolled from an industrial sized refrigerator; above, a fan turned slowly, spreading the smell of savory cooking. Celsa breathed deeply.

"*Mamá* is a great cook," she said. "She's an even better weaver, but she has no time. Never any time." She smacked the counter with her hand as they passed through.

His own mom would be in heaven in a kitchen like this, Angel thought. Did the desert hold enough hidden riches buy this for her?

Celsa led him silently out into the main hallway. Up a wide stairway, they could hear a woman's voice loudly singing to the radio. The dull drone of a vacuum cleaner almost drowned her out.

"This way," Celsa whispered.

Noiselessly they crossed the hall. Celsa opened a heavy wooden door into a large office and gestured for Angel to hurry in.

The room glowed with polished wood and leather. Books lined one wall. Windows opened to the blooming gardens on another. An expensive-looking computer sat on a big mahogany desk, its sleek shape out of place with the old wood and leather furniture. Behind the desk, a huge map of the Turquoise Hill Ranch nearly covered the wall. Angel and Celsa circled around until they stood in front of it, and stared.

"See…" Celsa motioned to the dozens of tiny colored markers that showed the location of herds, mines, roads, buildings, and the movement of ranch hands. Her finger moved slowly across the clusters of markers toward the upper quarter of the map.

Nothing. Nothing but the elevations and rivers. The land was utterly empty of any smudge of human life. In the center of that emptiness, lay the sacred mountain. With a shiver, Angel realized that this was the landscape of his dreams. With one hand, he gripped his two headed turquoise dragon. With the other, his finger traced the journey he remembered – the ancient trail to the kiva…

He hears distant chanting, songs pleading for the help of spirits as death prowls among the people. He feels the surge of desperate hope… Cradled in his arms lies the daughter of Tieholtsodi…and there is a chance of life again…The people call to him to join them…and he is there, wheeling above the clouds…looking down at the vast lands…

"What are you doing?" Celsa dug sharp fingers into his arm. He dropped the talisman. Like a radio snapped off, the chanting stopped.

Celsa looked at him, eyes widened. "*Oye!* You were blue again." Her voice cracked. "A blue light came out of the mouths of that snake thing and it was spreading all over you…What is happening? It's… it's magic, isn't it? It's the desert magic the old aunties and uncles talk about."

Magic! Holding the talisman with both hands, Angel lifted it up in front of him. A soft pulse matched his own heartbeat. This turquoise carving rippled with Anasazi magic… something to do with the turquoise egg…the daughter of Tieholtsodi…the magic the boy brought back to the kiva.

The magic was making him remember. *He is remembering everything…*

The door to the study flew open. Celsa's mother stood in the entrance, hands jammed on her hips.

"Celsa Reyna!" she exclaimed. A flood of angry Spanish followed. Angel dropped the talisman, instantly losing his lifeline to the old memories. Instead he felt his face burn even though he had no idea what was being said – except that Celsa was in a lot of trouble. His friend snapped back a sharp answer. In rapid Spanish, she and her mother exchanged arguments and a lot of infuriated hand wavings.

"I am ashamed!" Ana finally announced. "Angel, I am sorry. Celsa knows better and should not have brought you into *señor* Hydemann's office." She turned to her daughter and said sharply. "If you want to show your friend the map of the ranch, you ask *señor* Hydemann to show it. This is not our house!"

"Nothing is ours!" Celsa burst out. "*Nada y nada y nada*! Nothing! You don't have to tell me any more. I know. I know that everything is not ours! But it will be, *Mamá*. You might not believe it, but we will be rich too!"

Angel held his breath. He thought Ana might slap Celsa, but instead she swooped on her daughter and caught her up in a big hug. "We are rich – we have everything we need! We have each other and we have good hearts. That is enough."

Celsa rolled her eyes but she hugged her mother fiercely. "No, *Mamá*! Our own house, *Papá's* business, time for you to weave and a college fund – that would be enough."

"No one has an easy life. No one." Ana sighed. "Shoo, now. Go get your friend a snack from the kitchen. Boys his age, I know, are always hungry."

"Are you sure *señor* Hydemann can spare that?" Celsa shot back.

This time her mother did swat the girl on the bottom as she passed. "*Señor* Hydemann gave us two dollars for every one we saved for Jenny. And he works in the mud and heat just like your *Papá* and brothers. He paid the doctor bills for *Tía* Junie's twins and she doesn't even work for him. He is a good, generous man and you will be respectful!"

Celsa marched down the hall then spun around. "I'm sorry, *Mamá*," she tossed back, "but I am tired of being poor!"

Ana shook her head. "And maybe *señor* Hydemann is tired of being alone? What good is this big house when no one you love is in it with you? I feel sorry for *señor* Hydemann. You think about that, Celsa!"

"That's what she always says," Celsa muttered as the two of them went into the big kitchen. "And I don't see what good our family is when we're too poor to do anything but work."

Angel didn't bother answering. What good is a crummy motel, he thought, when no one in it loves you? Ana was right about that, even if Celsa didn't get it. And everybody, including rich Mr. Hydemann worked all the time. Everyone worked, Angel thought, except Gary.

Celsa just didn't know how good she had it with her brothers and sister and mother and father and Uncle Ramos and Auntie Junie and the twins. And what about Mr. John Hydemann who had no family – not even a sick mom? No one at all…

Angel scowled. Well, too bad for rich Mr. Hydemann. Maybe if he didn't hold so tight to all his land and money, he would have somebody.

In the kitchen, while Celsa examined the possibilities in the fridge, Angel ran his fingertips across the bump in his shirt made by his talisman and looked out the wide window. Even over the stale odor of air conditioning and the tasty aroma of a simmering stew, he could smell the scents of blooming flowers and acrid dust.

His heart longed to be out there…to be part of the free magic…

"Angel!" Celsa shrieked in his ear.

He turned reluctantly, letting go of the dragon. Her face was white.

"You were glowing again," she whispered. "What is happening to you?"

"Nothing," he muttered. "Nothing's happening!"

She yanked the string holding his amulet, pulling it from beneath his shirt. "It's that turquoise thing. It's doing something to you! You've got to get rid of it."

"No," Angel grabbed it from her hands and stepped back.

"It's a bad thing! Can't you see that it's putting some kind of spell on you!" Celsa reached for it again, but Angel pushed her hand away.

"Shut up!" Angel shouted. "It was my father's! So just *shut up!*"

It was then that Mr. Hydemann came into the kitchen.

His face was grey with exhaustion, his clothes grimed with dried mud and sweat. He smelled of cattle, dust and tired rancher. Eying the two teens standing stricken before him, he reached past Celsa into the fridge for a pitcher of iced tea. His face bland, he poured himself a large glass, but his eyes fastened on the turquoise dragon against Angel's chest.

Mr. Hydemann swallowed a large mouthful and ran his sleeve over his forehead, smearing dust and sweat across the white band of skin left by his hat.

"That's a very unusual carving," he said.

Angel gripped the amulet tightly. Despite the question's casual tone, the boy clearly heard the rancher's taut curiosity.

"His father gave it to him," Celsa blurted out, clearly flustered. "He just said so…" she faltered as Angel shot her a burning scowl.

"Curious." The rancher took another mouthful of iced tea. "Where'd your father get it?"

"Dunno," Angel muttered. He stuffed the dragon back under his shirt.

"Did he buy it in one of the tourist shops?" Mr. Hydemann took a step toward him, like Celsa, his fingers reaching for the carving.

Angel bolted. He slammed out of the kitchen door and tore past the pool and patio, into his own desert.

"Angel! *Wait!*" the rancher shouted. Angel kept going, didn't look back to see if Mr. Hydemann was chasing him. He hardly wondered if the rancher was going to complain to Gary. He just ran, like coyote, like jack rabbit, like road runner – like the desert animals fleeing danger.

Somewhere during his pounding run back toward the motel, his decision was made. When he leaped over the fence back onto the motel property, he veered toward the shed. Treese had said her brother's old camping stuff was out here.

Angel waded through boxes of old receipts, worn towels where rodents had nested, and into the very back of the shed. A couple of boxes with scrawled labels were shoved in a corner....*Will's stuff.*

They were heavy, but Angel pulled them to a clearer spot in the shed and ripped them open. Inside he found what he had hoped for – a camper's cooking kit that folded into itself so it wasn't much bigger than a small dinner plate. A big canteen and a large knife in a belt sheath lay farther down. A waterproof pack for matches was still full. A big, emerald green rucksack was shoved in the bottom. Angle hauled it out. The leather straps for fastening ground sheets and blankets were worn out and spots stained the fabric, but the pack looked sturdy.

Angel beat the dust and dead bugs out of the equipment and prowled through the rest of the boxes. He flipped through a small book about edible desert plants and added it to his equipment pile – could he live off the land like the animals? There was a dusty first aid kit with sealed bandages. He took the bandages and left the box.

He hid all but the cooking kit and canteen under a pile of boxes; these, he stuffed in an old paper bag, and then with a quick look to be sure no one was around, sprinted to the back door of the motel. He could see Treese in the office registering a trucker for the night, so he slipped into the bathroom and locked the door. He scrubbed out the canteen and dishes. Mostly they were sticky with spider webs and dust.

Returning to his room, he pushed the gear to the back of his closet. Making sure Treese was still busy out front, Angel methodically went through the storage cupboards. From the linens storeroom he helped himself to two of the oldest blankets from a pile that hardly ever got used. In the pantry, he grabbed some cans of tuna, chili and soup.

"That you, Angel?" Treese called.

Angel jumped, then forced his voice calm. He stepped into the hall where she could see him. "Yeah?"

"Gary's bringin' pizza for dinner," Treese said over her shoulder as the front door swung open again. "Could you get some extra towels and an ashtray down to number 5? Thanks, Angel."

Angel hid the pilfered food in his closet, and then ran the towels and supplies to the motel room. He had wanted to be ready before Gary got back, but he needed more food. His foster father was as shrewd as a rat and Angel was terrified that the man would catch on.

But luck favored him in the motel room. The trucker was a real nice man with a son he was lonesome for. While he chatted, Angel spotted the trash can stacked up with empty water bottles.

"Let me empty that trash for you," Angel offered. There were four big bottles – he would have water in the desert.

Quick as anything, he took out the containers he needed, dropped them into the shadows by the back door, and emptied the garbage in the dumpster. Through the screen, Angel could see Treese chatting with one of their guests. Driven by fear that Gary would get back before he was ready, Angel ran the empty trash can to the trucker's room, and then dashed again to the motel bathroom, slowing only to grab the water bottles. Rapidly, he rinsed and filled them. With a flash of panic, he wondered if somehow the stash in his closet might be seen if Treese came into his room. He had to get his gear farther away. Treese was checking in a family with three kids – all jumping around and demanding pop from the machine. She'd be calling him to run errands soon for sure. The shed. They never went there.

"*Angel!*" Treese called from the office. "*Number 14 needs a cot brought in.*"

"Sure thing," Angel called back. "I'll take it over right away."

"*Thanks!*"

But instead of going for the cot, Angel feverishly filled the bag with water, gear and food cans and clutching it under his arm, sprinted to the shed and shoved it into the backpack, then hid the whole thing behind a heap of boxes and old car parts. Breathing hard, he checked out the area – nobody in sight. With relief prickling his neck, he hurried back to the motel and pushed the cot from the storage room down to number 14. He was just coming out when Gary's pick-up wheeled into the parking lot. His foster father jumped out balancing a big pizza box and a twelve-pack of beer.

All the better if Gary drank himself to sleep tonight, Angel thought. He was ready. He was finally ready.

But then, Mr. John Hydemann's big car drove into the parking lot.

FIFTEEN

Angel had no time to get away before the rancher caught sight of him. Gary's eyes followed Hydemann's gaze to where Angel tried to slide back into the shadows.

"Well, come on, boy," Gary called out. "Pizza's gonna get cold."

For a panicked minute, Angel thought of running. But there was no use. He might be able to escape the rancher, but he knew Gary could run him down. Reluctantly, he walked toward the men, furious with himself for getting caught.

"Good to see you, John," Gary said, suspicion shading his voice. "How about a beer?"

Mr. Hydemann didn't bother to smile. "Thanks, but no." He watched Angel approaching. "I didn't finish a chat I was having with Angel this afternoon."

"Has he done something?" Gary demanded. "I told him to stay clear…"

Angel saw the narrowing of his foster father's eyes. Dangerous.

"No, not at all," the rancher said. "I was curious about that carving he has – the two-headed snake. Looks valuable to me."

"It is?" Gary put the pizza on the hood of his truck and the beer on the ground. "Let's see that thing, Angel," he commanded.

In a flood of fury, Angel raised his fists. "It was my father's and now it's mine. Don't you think of touching it, Gary!"

He didn't hear Treese come out of the motel office.

"Why you …" Gary growled.

Angel backed up fast, and ran smack into Treese.

"It's okay, Mr. Tanner. Let it be." Mr. Hydemann's voice was a half a tone short of a command. "I collect Native American antique artifacts and I thought maybe your son had acquired one, somehow. It's just a professional interest."

"It's mine," Angel said, breathing hard. "I didn't find it or steal it. Some people have their own stuff!"

"You pipe down," Gary snapped. "So are you offering to buy, John? Show it, Angel!" He reached out and gripped Angel's shoulder, digging in his fingers, yanking him forward.

Trapped, Angel slowly took out the talisman. If he hadn't, he was sure Gary would rip it from his neck. The greed of the man who had everything and the man who wanted everything would find a way to get his birthright if he wasn't really careful.

The dragon gleamed sky blue in his hand.

Mr. Hydemann stepped closer, not touching, just looking. His eyes searched out Angel's. "Where'd you get this, son?" he asked.

"I ain't your son," Angel said. He tried to twist away, but Gary gripped his shoulder too tightly.

"Are you interested in buying?" Gary repeated.

Mr. Hydemann took out his wallet. "A thousand dollars," he said. "I'll give you a thousand for it. Right now. Or double, if you'll take a check."

"No!" Angel stuffed the dragon back under his shirt and despite Gary, folded his arms over his chest.

"Well …" Gary let go of Angel's shoulder, greed gleaming in his eyes.

"It belongs to Angel," Treese interrupted. "That thing don't belong to Gary or me, Mr. Hydemann. So if Angel don't want to sell it, that's all there is to it."

"I won't sell it," Angel said, breathing hard. "I won't."

The rancher frowned and reluctantly stepped back before Treese's glare. "Okay," he said. "But if you change your mind, Angel…if anyone else offers to buy it, I'd be really grateful if you'd come to me first. I'll match anyone's price. That's a promise. Will you shake on that?"

Treese bumped Angel's shoulder, and so he shook the calloused hand of the rancher. At the last second the boy looked up, remembering too late, the effect his blue eyes had on the man.

The rancher gripped his hand tightly for a moment longer. An emotion Angel couldn't identify flickered across his face. Then it was over.

Once the rancher drove off, Treese took the pizza and Gary picked up the beer.

"You are such a loser," Gary told Angel. "You whine about your poor sick mama, but when you got a chance to get some real money you just can't do it, can you? You really are pathetic, kid."

"Gary," Treese said. "Can't you just shut up for once?"

"Ho," Gary shot back. "You're gettin' a bit cranky, ain'tcha?" He grinned. "But just you wait, Treese Tanner. Things are gonna be happenin' around here!"

They went into the motel, side by side. Feeling like the heart in his chest had turned into a lump of raw turquoise, Angel followed.

Sprawled on his bed, Angel stared out the open window at the moon drifting across the ink-stained sky. Sounds of the desert seeped into the room. His heart thumped slowly, powerfully in his chest. He waited.

The evening was taking forever. Gary had gone on being jubilant and mysterious, dropping crude hints about turquoise and fast cash while they ate pizza. At first Angel felt sick with relief that Gary wasn't trying to sell the dragon talisman. Then he turned just as sick with worry that his foster father had found his mine or even Celsa's Anasazi ruins. And all the while, underneath his anxiety, another emotion was building – one that made him feel as if his eyes were blazing and his muscles were getting ready to leap across the table at Gary. He felt like a powerful desert predator – a mountain lion maybe. But his head said that that trying to act as tough and fierce as a cougar would be a really dumb move. So when the pizza was eaten, Angel retreated to his bedroom.

His fingers played over the dragon, thinking about what Gary had said. "I won't let you down, Mom," he whispered. He wouldn't sell his dragon, so he'd have to find another way to get the money.

Twisting restlessly, he held the amulet up to the moonlight. If the carving was some kind of magnet for old Anasazi magic, maybe he could use it to find the hidden turquoise mines. Maybe that blue light gave him powers of some kind – like getting Mr. Hydemann's car to whack Gary, or persuading snakes to go away, or lifting a rock that he shouldn't be able to budge.

No wonder Mr. Hydemann wanted his dragon amulet – he must've known about the magic. Magic. His own desert magic, given to him by his mysterious father. And all Angel had to do was figure out how to use its power.

Thrumming with energy, Angel sat up.

How should he start? After thinking about it for a minute, he crossed his legs and dropped his hands over his knees the way he'd seen on TV shows. Closing his eyes, he tried to breathe deeply and evenly.

"Magic come to me," he whispered. He opened one eye to see if there was any blue glow spreading over his skin. Nothing. He shut his eyes again and tried to concentrate.

In the next room, a chair scraped. A country music song shattered the short silence as the radio was switched on. Angel's eyes flew open again. Taking another deep breath, he tried to relax his twanging nerves. An announcer shouted out that his cars were the cheapest. Music blared. There was a lot of movement and banging. Then laughing.

Angel's breath hissed between his teeth. He slid off the bed and opened the door just enough to peer toward the kitchen. Gary had shoved the table against the wall and he and Treese were dancing to the fast beat of the music. Treese laughed when Gary shimmied down, a beer bottle held up in one hand.

Stepping back into his room, Angel pressed his forehead against the door frame. This place was stopping him – it was all wrong. The dragon was desert magic. He would have to go into the desert to awaken its powers.

Silently, he crept from his room, eased down the hall and went into the storage room where a big window faced the desert. The music was still blasting when he shoved open the pane. It squealed. Angel held his breath. The singing and thumping kept up in the kitchen.

Boosting himself over the sill, he dropped to the ground below. He landed hard and took a second to catch his breath; then running low, so that none of the lights coming from the motel windows would catch him, Angel sped across the hard packed dirt. The shed loomed ghostly pale in the moonlight. He yanked the door open. The hinges shrieked, the sound cracking the night. Angel swung the rucksack on his back and leaving the door ajar, turned toward the moon-lit desert. Taking the sagging wire fence at a bound, he loped as easily as a coyote across the rolling landscape.

His senses took it all in – soft wingbeats of flying creatures, skittering feet of small animals, a single cry as a predator made its kill. The cooling wind brought all the scents to his flared nostrils. This was his home. This was his place.

When he reached the standing rock that concealed his cache, his breath had hardly quickened beyond soft panting. He dropped down and again sat cross-legged, back straight against the stone. Gazing across the landscape, he saw with quiet wonder that the cactus and rocks were as clear to him as if moonlight, grown strong with magic, shone incandescent in the sky. He raised his eyes to the night. In silky blackness, stars blazed and danced. He knew those dances.

Eyes open, he breathed slowly and evenly. With both hands he touched the talisman against his chest...

A cry of grief ululates through the night. The boy runs from one body to another...touching their wounds...their pock-marked skin. The precious egg lies on the ground, forgotten.

The boy is choking on his anger and despair. The enemies will pay! He seizes his atlatl and shakes the spear at the distant stars. From the cold campfire he daubs black ash across his chest and face.

He hunts...with the cunning of coyote...the stealth of gray fox...the ferocity of eagle...the enemies will pay.

Through the night he runs to the kivas of the enemies. Too late... the people are gone, but their treasures remain. The boy smashes pots, slashes blankets, throws turquoise into the cold embers of their campfires...but the enemies do not return. In the end, he stands alone in the dull twilight of empty dawn. No living thing but the hissing siblings of Tieholtsodi's daughter are with him.

He throws back his head and cries to the sun and moon the depth of his grief. He is alone.

The Anasazi boy's cry of anguish echoed in his mind and heart. Shoving his knuckles into his mouth to keep himself silent, Angel's chest rose and fell. He knew such loss.

What had happened to the people? Did they all starve? Did their enemies kill them? Was it a big sickness?

Sitting alone in the desert night, Angel looked up at the piercing stars. That boy had walked this land – had smelled the same scents, heard the same sounds, felt the same wind on his face. Angel touched the talisman again. It was a true link to the boy.

A coyote yipped. The sweet dry land crowded his senses. It was his home. For a long time Angel sat quietly, bathing himself in the desert.

His plans grew like a desert plant after rain. He would not live in exile any longer.

Filled with wild excitement, he stood up, stamped the blood through his limbs and ran silently back to the motel. It seemed easy somehow to scale the wall and catapult into the open window of the storage room. The place was dark. Gary snored loudly, then softer. Angel eased into the kitchen and stopped cold. Gary must've gotten really drunk. By the blue light of the motel's neon sign, he saw the safe door in the office was smashed. The metal box of turquoise nuggets had been broken open and the stones thrown across the floor.

Angel's nostrils flared in fierce greed. Crouching amid the scattered gemstones, he touched them with splayed fingers. He could take every single one and serve Gary right. And the jerk couldn't turn Angel into the cops or Mrs. Preston, because this turquoise had been stolen from John Hydemann. Angel's tongue darted over his lips. It was perfect!

But as he touched the stones, he heard Treese mutter in her sleep. If both Angel and the turquoise disappeared, she would get the brunt of Gary's anger. Angel's grasping hand dropped and then reached out again. Instead of scooping handfuls, he took only his own six stones, still knotted in the frayed bandana.

Soft-footed, Angel returned to the kitchen. With cautious motions he opened cupboards and the fridge, carefully selecting as much food as he thought he could carry for his journey. Treese wouldn't begrudge it to him, so it wasn't stealing. But then at the last minute, Angel unknotted the bandana and took out a small stone. Wrapping it in a screw of paper, he dropped it in her Tweetie Bird mug.

With the food, some warm clothes and his pocketknife stuffed into his old backpack, he climbed back out of the storage room window. Running low past the shed, he wished he had mining tools, even a pick.

No matter what you got, you want something else, he thought. His mom had always said that wanting was a sure way to be unhappy.

There was almost no unhappiness in him right now. As the desert night wrapped around him, he felt nothing but fierce joy. He would lose himself in the desert until he had enough turquoise or Anasazi treasure to save his mom. Too bad for Gary and too bad for Mr. John Hydemann. Nothing was going to stop him. Nothing.

SIXTEEN

By the time the glow of sunrise washed the horizon, Angel had covered several miles. At his cache, he had transferred all his possessions into the rucksack, shouldered it and set out with a dogged, loping stride. As never before, he sensed the beating heart of the land. Above, bats winged by with silent cries. A bobcat squalled at him from the top of a rock outcropping. More than once, a coyote traveled through the dry brush only a few yards from his own path. A silent fox slipped by when he slowed his pace.

He saw them, heard them, and tasted their passing on the breeze. He was filled with pulsing energy. Like wavering flames in a well-used fire pit, the speech of the old ones flickered through his mind. Around him the desert's ghost voices chittered with excitement. Dust devils whirled in the still, pre-dawn air. *Ghosts...*

The early morning sun streaked the sky with vast swaths of red and gold as he climbed a weathered outcropping to survey the landscape. Behind him, the motel had dropped below the horizon line. To the southeast, the Turquoise Hill ranch house was hidden too, but the tops of windmills and old trees were visible. The desert air seemed miraculously clear – too clear. He could see all the details of the landscape – miles and miles of them.

Breath suddenly coming hard, Angel touched the talisman against his chest. It throbbed beneath his fingers. *The magic.* The magic was working, giving him sight as good as a wild animal – as good as an eagle. No...better! An eagle could see one or two miles clearly. He, Angel, was looking out over many miles – and every bush, every animal was clear in his sight.

Angel flicked his tongue over his lips. What was happening to him?

Terrified, he let go of the amulet. But nothing changed. He knew his eyes would be blazing blue, blue like turquoise. The noises around him were sharpening, getting clearer, louder...swirling words into his mind... calling him...*crazy*...

"No!" Angel screamed. He tore the amulet from his neck and threw it across the desert floor. But the voices didn't stop...now all his senses flared, exploding with images of life and movement and...age. Incredible age...

The scents, whispers and vivid colors flooded his mind, drowning his thoughts and fears, carrying him away...higher and higher...leaping and beating his way to the sky...wheeling on the wind...iridescent flashes...his brothers...his sisters...his cousins...higher and higher... dancing joy in the air...*too high...no...not now...not yet...*

Darkness, silent darkness...Screaming and screaming...Angel fell to the ground. Broken...everything broken in shrieking pain...hazy turquoise...warm burnt sugar wafting over his face...it was all gone...he couldn't...*he couldn't do it...*

"Angel..." The voice wavered in his hearing. "*Angel...wake up!*"

Water dripped into his mouth. Instinctively, Angel licked his lips, then his muscles spasmed in terror. *Falling... he was falling.* His eyes flew open.

Blue sky blazed behind a dark head. He thrashed weakly.

"Stay still," Celsa commanded. "I think you have sunstroke."

Angel groaned, tried to sit up, and then fell back. He felt bruised all over – the dream...the dream that he had fallen from the sky.

"Stay *still!*" Celsa repeated.

"No," he panted. With a grunt, he forced himself upright and looked around. Late afternoon, he guessed. Hours. He'd been unconscious for hours – caught in that terrifying dream of super senses. He sniffed the air – dry and clear and ordinary, not swirling with images. He flexed his arms – normal, not pulsing with extra strength. He squinted at a distant yellow-flowered chamisa bush. As the clarity of its outline faded with distance, Angel let out a sobbing breath. He wasn't crazy. He was back to normal.

"Drink some more," Celsa urged, holding a canteen out to him. He took it in shaky hands and swallowed several mouthfuls. His head was clearing now. Really clearing. Everything looked, smelled and sounded normal to him. Smelled and sounded...dull.

Don't go there, Angel, he thought fiercely. *Stay normal.*

"What are you doing here?" he asked thickly.

"*Oye!* Obviously saving your life," she replied. "It's a miracle I found you. There was this weird dust storm that came out of nowhere. It moved so slow, I was able to stay ahead of it, but it kept twisting and pushing at me. Just luck I ended up here. There was a coyote sniffing around you, even."

"Brother..." Angel said weakly, then flushed. Celsa would think he was crazy. "But why are you here?" he asked. He took in the wide hat shoved on her head, the dark school tee-shirt covered with an open red blouse, and the crammed backpack with an attached bedroll lying in the dust.

"Everyone's looking for you," she said. "*Señor* Hydemann was driving *mamá* and me into town for the week's groceries, and he wanted to talk to you – said he'd got you in trouble – so we pulled into the motel. I guess some lady from the state..."

"Mrs. Preston?" Angel interrupted.

Celsa nodded. "Yeah, that was her name. She was there. Treese and Gary had just found out you were gone. Gary was yelling that you stole from him and Treese was yelling at him and Mrs. Preston was yelling at both of them because you'd run away." Celsa grinned and sat back, fanning her hot face with her hand. "It was pretty funny. Everyone was yelling and no one was listening. And when we got out of the car, Treese started yelling at *señor* Hydemann for persecuting you and then *mamá* yelled at her."

"Wow!" Angel said. "Now I *know* I never want to go back. What did Mr. Hydemann do?"

Celsa frowned. "He talked to Mrs. Preston, and then he said he'd get some men and start searching for you."

"What?" Angel shouted. "Why are you sitting here talking? I've got to get away!" He scanned the horizon – other than a hawk winging high above, there was no sign of movement.

"Calm down." Celsa grabbed his shirt and pulled him back to a sitting position. "I told everyone you said you wanted to camp up by the Jemez River and then go see the turquoise mines. So that's where everyone's looking. It's *miles* from here." She frowned at him. "But I've got to ask you, Angel, were you running out on me?"

Angel looked into her dark, square face. "No…yes…I had to get away," he said. He hated the way his voice quavered.

Celsa shrugged, made a show of screwing the lid on her canteen. She stood and pointed west. "There's an arroyo over there. We can make camp and no one will see us. But," she turned fiercely on Angel, jabbing her finger toward him, "you remember I saved your life today, just like you saved mine. Out here people die when they can't depend on their partners! When you can't depend on someone's promise."

Angel felt the heat flushing his neck and face. "Celsa, I'm sorry. You've got to believe me. You can depend on me!"

"Yeah?" Celsa retorted. "I think you're going to have to prove that." She picked up her gear and trudged toward the arroyo. Stiffly, Angel picked up his own pack and followed her, kicking at small rocks along the way. A gleam of blue caught his eye. The amulet. He froze, and then with a rush of joy, scooped the talisman from the dust and hung it around his neck – where it belonged.

It took him a while to pick his way down the rough banks of the arroyo; his bones felt watery and his muscles unsure. At the bottom, Celsa had already chosen a campsite where an overhang of weathered rock shielded them from the slanting sun's rays. Without speaking, Angel sat down beside her with his back to the stone wall, his shoulder not touching hers, but he thought he could feel her warmth anyway. He hoped miserably that he hadn't ruined their friendship. His stomach growled – 24 hours since his last meal. Pulling open his pack, he dug out a small feast and arranged it in front of them both.

"Go on," he urged. "I have lots."

She nodded and picked up a piece of chicken. For several minutes they ate without letting their eyes meet.

Finally Celsa made a noise between a grunt and a sigh in her throat and elbowed Angel. "Want a brownie?" she asked.

"You brought brownies?" He relaxed into a grin of relief.

"Sí. Mi mamá made them this morning and I brought a couple. For a treat. She makes really good brownies." Celsa reached into in her pack, and with a deep chuckle, held out a mashed lump of chocolate to Angel. "They looked better this morning."

He laughed, relieved. "Thanks." He took it and scooped the crumbs into his mouth. "'S good…really good."

They relapsed into sleepy silence, by unspoken agreement staying where they were until the sun had almost set. As twilight crept over them, the land faded to blue gray and views were lost in shadow, but there was enough light to pack up and start out.

"Let's follow the arroyo for as long as we can," Celsa said. "It's heading the right way."

Angel rotated his shoulders, trying to stretch out his bruised and cramped shoulder muscles. He turned his face to the sacred mountain's hazy mass. "Our path is that way."

"*Si*, but I want to be sure." Celsa took out a compass and checked it, but Angel walked ahead. His feet knew the trail to the sacred mountain. The turquoise had come from there. Probably any lost Anasazi ruins would be there. Most of all, his heart told him that that was where the grandfather's voice had called from.

Ghost or craziness, he was going home. His heart sang with joy.

"Wait up," Celsa called. He hardly heard her. Dust devils swirled over the hummocks and in the brush behind them. As his senses quickened, he was aware of the life around him, of Celsa's footsteps thudding on the path.

"Angel!" Her voice pierced his rioting senses and he turned to her, deeply aware of the details of her hair and skin, the folds of her shirt, the scent of old sweat embedded in her hat...Beautiful, all beautiful and so alive.

"Angel..." she whispered again.

He simply gazed, feeling the waves of life rising around him – *through* him. He heard his brothers calling him, pulling his eyes heavenward.

Whack! Her hand smacked his face as hard as Gary had ever done. He blinked, too shocked to be angry, and stepped back.

"Why...What are you doing?" he demanded, hand clapped to his face.

"*Stop it!*" she yelled. Startled, he saw she had tears in her eyes. "Stop it, Angel!"

"What?" He rubbed his cheek. She had really put some muscle behind the slap. "Why did you hit me? Are you still mad or something?" He was too bewildered to be angry.

"You...you were blue. All glowing blue...and your eyes were getting really weird. Really crazy looking."

"No, I wasn't! It was just…it was just…" He turned away, humiliation and fear rushing over him. Was it happening to him like it had to his mother? He had to fight it. He couldn't give in to craziness. If he did…if he lost himself like she had, it was all over for him and no hope left for her. He wouldn't give in. He wouldn't. But the fear made his knees weak.

He crouched down and ran his hands through hair. Celsa squatted in front of him. Gently, she reached out and laid a hand on his knee, warm and comforting. With her other hand she touched his cheek.

"What is it?" she demanded. "You have to tell me. Remember, partners depend on each other. They *trust* each other."

Great – except he couldn't trust himself. With tears pricking at his eyes, Angel leaped to his feet and backed away. "Well, maybe I don't want to be partners," he panted. "Just leave me alone!"

He turned and strode away, pointing himself at the sacred mountain. He would go home! *Home!*

"Angel, think!" he groaned, forcing himself to stop his headlong rush toward the mountain.

He had been having hallucinations. Maybe he was getting lost in madness like his mom. And now he was trying to get to where all the craziness came from? *Home. Going home.*

He sank down into the dust again. The closer he got to the mountain, the crazier he was getting. But it was too late. He couldn't go back – Gary would kill him. Mrs. Preston would take him away to some "safe" institution. And he had been beyond crazy to think he could come out here in the desert and live like what? A coyote?

Celsa came striding up to him and this time slammed a punch into his shoulder.

"Ow!" Angel yelled. "Leave me alone!"

"Oh, yeah sure! *'I keep my promises,'*" she mimicked. "What are you *doing*? Are you *loco*? Are you trying to kill us both? You can't go running around in the desert like it's a park! And you…and you *left me!*"

She sat down hard beside him, squeezed tight against herself. Her shoulders shook and she turned her face away.

Hot with shame, Angel took a deep breath. "I won't…I won't do it again."

"*Si!* You promise and then you forget. You just forget. Out here, that can make me dead!' Her voice was flat. Ashamed, Angel let his shoulder lean against hers, savoring the human warmth. He reached for her hand but she shook him off. Celsa sniffed softly then became silent too.

Angel felt the talisman around his neck. Was it was the source of the desert magic? Was it seeping into him the way dust seeped into his hair and clothes and shoes, coating his ears and nostrils as he breathed it in with each living breath. How much of him, of Angel, was being absorbed by desert dust?

Is that what happened to his mother? She had said once a long time ago that everything changed for her when she had become lost in the desert and hiked, half dead with thirst, to the sacred mountain. She said she had found a desert spirit living there, that he had saved her and together they had created their son. Angel looked in the direction of the mountain that was pulling him like a magnet. He shivered.

"I won't leave you," he said at last to Celsa. "I don't forget my promises – not to anyone." Tentatively he put his arm around her shoulders. She stiffened and then abruptly leaned against him. He swallowed and dropped a kiss on her cheek. His promise for real.

She pushed him away, but Angel could see the smile flitting across her face as she stood. "Okay, then. We'd better get going."

SEVENTEEN

The dried streambed curved slightly like a long, lazy snake slinking through the grey dusk. The moon had sailed free of the land and shone down on them, making the desert glitter with black and white magic. Cottonwoods rustled in the breeze. Angel and Celsa hiked wearily along the arroyo.

When the streambed snaked south, they climbed out and turned due west, hiking over the rolling landscape. Ahead, the sacred mountain rose like a brooding spirit. Despite the moonlight, thunderheads were banking on its flank – bursts of lightning crackling to the desert floor. To Angel, it looked like the spirits of his grandfather's warriors hurling their atlatls in some ancient, wild hunt.

"*Hay-ya-yay!* Those are some storm clouds," Celsa murmured. "We'll have to watch for flooding."

Angel grunted assent. The wild feeling was growing on him again, but he wasn't giving into it. They were hiking into wilder country now; dry stream beds wound between spires of rocks, criss-crossing the land. Several times they had to skirt stands of wicked cactus or climb down the steep crumbly arroyo banks into inky shadows below, and then somehow find a path up again. Angel took the lead, giving Celsa a hand along the rougher parts.

She slipped once and cried out, cutting the sound off with a snap.

"Y'okay?" Angel asked. He reached his hand to her, and pulled her closer to him. She moved away, but slowly.

"It's fine," she said. "Thorn in my hand. It's okay."

Angel peered ahead. Rocks and rolling hillocks loomed before them. Cliffs and bluffs reared in the distance. Above that, the moon had been slowly swallowed by thunderheads, making the dark landscape harder to cross on foot. Imperceptibly at first, then stronger, blending with the beating of his heart, Angel became aware of drums reaching out to him across the desert, across time. Showing him the way. Angel breathed a silent prayer to the grandfather. As the words rose in his heart, his sight, hearing and smell grew sharper. Instinctively, his feet knew the way they needed to go.

He clenched his teeth. Okay, so he was getting Indian magic vision – he'd use it. But he would control it – he'd never let it control him again.

"I think I can see the way," he said softly.

"*Bien*," Celsa grunted, "because I can hardly see anything." She shone a pencil flashlight briefly on her compass. "We're still heading west."

Angel smiled. He could see the rugged terrain as clearly as the heroes in those spy movies who wore infra-red goggles. And the mountain sang out to him. Suddenly, he wondered if he was not being crazy, but maybe turning into something special – like a super hero with super powers.

The idea tugged on his mind; it would sure serve Gary right if his "nothin'" foster son turned out to be someone after all. A hero. Somebody that everybody looked up to. Important. Rich. Like John Hydemann; not like Gary. What would it be like to be special?

"Slow down, Angel," Celsa hissed.

Still picturing Gary making up to him, asking for favors, Angel waited. Celsa limped up, stumbling and breathing hard. When she stopped beside him and wiped her sleeve over her damp forehead, he looked at her in concern and handed her a bottle of water.

"*Gracias*. Wish I could use the flashlight," she said. "I keep stumbling on rocks. My leg's a bit stiff and I'm afraid I'll sprain my ankle – that would really mess things up."

As she chugged the water, she watched him closely. Angel didn't like it, so he turned away. "Why don't we take a break over there," he said, pointing to a low bluff. "The rocks have ledges – we can sit down." Despite the poor light, he could clearly see the striated levels where sand and wind had worn smooth ledges in the stone, much like a tier of benches.

"Let's go, then." Celsa's voice was ragged with exhaustion. This time when he held out a steadying hand, she took it.

At the ledge, they sat silently, drinking slowly from their stash of water. Angel's eyes were pulled upward by wingbeats he could hear far above them. He wanted to call out to the creatures up there. He stood, and without thinking raised his arms to them. He could hear the voices...

A shock of water hit him full in the face.

"What!" he spluttered.

Celsa pushed him back against the rock wall. She held her canteen ready to throw more water on him. "Are you okay, now?" she asked, her voice level.

The wingbeats faded...the voices hushed.

"Yeah. Thanks." Angel couldn't believe he had nearly lost it again. If Celsa hadn't yanked him back what would've happened? The rock at his back was twenty feet high. What if he'd climbed it and thought he could fly? *Again. Would he survive a second time...had he fallen...had he dreamed?*

"We'd better keep going," Celsa interrupted his thoughts.

"Wait!" She turned, eyebrows raised, but Angel didn't know what to say. Finally he stammered out, "I'm not really weird."

"Oh, no. Nothing weird about you." She heaved her backpack over her shoulders. "At least when your eyes glow, you can see the path."

"My eyes are glowing?" He could hear the panic in his own voice.

"Like a pair of blue lasers," she said wearily. "How else do you think I followed you in the dark? Can I hold on to you? I might not fall so much."

Angel held out his hand and was reassured when Celsa gripped it. Aware that she was losing strength, he searched ahead for the smoothest path.

Thrumming chants walked with him, but they filled him with strength. He could walk, run if he wanted to, for hours. Celsa kept the pace, grunting sometimes when she banged into a rock or a scratching plant. Not complaining.

"We should stop," he urged her during a brief break.

"No, not while we are too close to any possible search parties," she said hoarsely. Angel nodded and kept going, supporting her when she needed it.

Toward sunrise, Angel decided they had to make camp or the searchers would for sure find them collapsed with exhaustion, or worse. Celsa's breathing was labored, and off to the east, storm clouds were stacking sullenly against the sky. Sheets of gray rain hid the distant landscape. Splinters of lightning occasionally crackled from sky to ground. Wind gusted, dry and hot, prickling their skin and choking them with blowing dust.

"Looks like some caves up ahead," Angel said. "Can you make another half mile or so?"

"*Sí*," Celsa hissed. "But we'll have to be careful." She pointed to the shadow of rain falling against the mountain. "There's going to be flooding."

A rumble of thunder punctuated her words. Dust devils flew erratically in all directions, driven by gusts of wind.

"I'll find us some safe shelter," Angel promised.

"Use those laser eyes and see through solid stone," she retorted.

It took less time than he'd expected. Without realizing it, they had gained elevation. The limestone rock was weathered with pockets, ledges and caves. Ancient geological events had piled rocks atop one another, reddish and white, creating magnificent sculptures of stone, all laid against desert and sky.

"Why don't you wait here," Angel said. "I'll find us something. Sit down and take it easy."

Celsa shook her head. "If I sit now, I won't get up. You go ahead, and I'll just follow a little slower."

Angel nodded and jogged ahead. Rather than his strength waning with exhaustion, waves of energy seared through Angel's muscles and bones. His body had become hard like rock, fluid like water, light like air, and blazing like flame. Utterly alive.

He scrambled over jumbled stones and swiftly climbed the rock face, at last finding a shelter that suited him. About ten feet off the desert floor, a shallow cave had been gouged by endless years of buffeting wind and sand. All around the cave, other bowl-shaped pockets had been eroded into the limestone wall. Dried sticks, plant matter and old bones gave evidence that the desert wildlife had made good use of the sites for their own housing. But for now, it was deserted.

He climbed up and stood on the small ledge, waving to Celsa. She lifted her head and plodded slowly toward him. At the foot, she stood a moment, head down. Then with a deep breath she grabbed the handholds in the cliff and hoisted herself up. Angel slid down beside her, steadying and supporting her as she made her way to the cave. With a sigh of utter exhaustion, Celsa sank onto the rocky floor.

"Finally," she muttered. "I didn't think I was in such bad shape."

"You did great," Angel said. He offered her another bottle of water and the last piece of chicken.

"I can't eat," she sighed. "Just water..."

She gulped it down and then crawled a few feet inside the cave. "Home sweet home." Dropping her pack, she laid her head on the bundle; in less than a minute, she was snoring.

Angel watched her for a moment, thinking how soft and vulnerable she looked. Who would have guessed the rock-hard determination inside her? He wondered if he too should sleep. But energy still washed through him like the floods in the arroyos, so he sat cross-legged at the front of the cave overlooking the desert. The land spread out before him, silent and beautiful. He sat without moving, watching the sun climb white-hot into the sky beyond the grey clouds. At last, he ate the chicken and an orange, and then lay down with his head cradled on his pack, his face turned toward the land and sky.

He sighed in contentment and felt himself drifting into sleep...

The world spreads below him like a quilt rumpled over an unmade bed. He feels the strength of his shoulders, the muscles rippling along his back and chest as his wings beat through cool air. On either side, above and below, the dragons swirl through air and clouds, climbing, diving, and roaring with joy. To Angel's eyes, they shimmer every shade of blue, green and turquoise – almost invisible against the early morning light.

In his mind, he hears their singing, feels their delight that he is flying with them at last. Part of him wants only to soar with them, but something nags at his thoughts.

"This is a fantastic dream," rolls through his mind.

He circles over the ledge in front of the cave where Celsa sleeps. His backpack lies where he left it. Weird. He thought he'd see his sleeping form lying on top of the pack. It troubles him that this dream isn't unfolding the way he thinks dreams should.

One dragon, larger, deeper blue than the rest, leaves the swooping pack and circles around him.

"Angel," it hisses.

Angel doesn't bother to answer, just beat his wings, climbing toward the mountainous clouds. The winds inside the thunderhead nearly roll him over. Lightning ricochets at every side. He dives and soars on the wild winds, and then he breaks through to golden light. The warmth is wonderful. The blue dragon's wings beat the air behind him.

"Angel," it calls.

Again, Angel ignores the beast. Can he fly all the way to the sun? He laughs at the thought. Fire shoots from his mouth, rolling and crackling like a ball of lightning. He does it again, roaring in joy. He thrusts his wings hard and soars past the edge of the thunderhead to where he can see the land spread out beneath him. A moving puff of dust catches his eye. Lazily he sweeps toward it. A truck. Gary's truck. Heading toward the caves where Celsa sleeps. The truck backfires, sending a plume of dirty smoke into the clean air. The smell of bad gas puffs into his nostrils, sharp and hard. He sneezes.

Sneezes! No one sneezes in a dream...

It wasn't a dream. Gary's truck was real!

Angel circled high above, watching. His clear vision saw the shovels and picks bouncing in the back of the vehicle, the rifle attached to the gun rack. Another acrid puff of fuel exhaust assaulted his nostrils. Frantic, Angel winged toward the caves. Gary was heading straight for them – straight to where Angel's green backpack sat up on the ledge, so bright that even a fool like Gary wouldn't miss it.

Angel backswept his wings, pausing high in the air. How did he know to do this? What was he going to do? If he tried to land on the ledge, Gary would see him. Celsa would probably scream – and he would fall off. This dragon body was a lot bigger than his boy body. Was he completely insane?

Around him, other dragons still soared against the sky, their iridescent scales making them invisible to the unclear eyes of humans.

Angel peered downward, thinking, forcing himself to think. Dragon recklessness coursed through him...he had to think...he could get away, fly higher and higher... he had to save Celsa. Gary...a snarl curled Angel's lips. His tongue flicked out, tasting the air. Why was Gary out here? Not looking for Angel. Turquoise. Gary was mining turquoise. But where?

Angel circled widely, searching the vast landscape. The mountain. Gary's turquoise came from the sacred mountain – it had to be. There was no other place that Hydemann or the local tribes wouldn't have already mined.

Gary was crazy – really crazy. Mining the sacred mountain was like robbing a church. The tribes wouldn't stand for it. And Hydemann would haul Gary through the legal system until it was a sure thing Gary would never get out of prison.

Gary had to know the risk he was taking. He wouldn't let anyone in on a secret like this. He wouldn't let anyone walk away with his secret.

Angel circled again. The emerald backpack practically glowed in the desert light. What would Gary do if he found Celsa out here? If he found Angel, the boy – or even Angel, the dragon. What would a rifle shell do to a dragon's flesh?

The blue dragon was circling him, hissing wildly. Angel couldn't understand...felt the strength drain from his shoulders...felt the wings seem to fade away. He was falling – wide awake and falling. No! Not now! *No!*

He screamed and his hands clawed the air. The blue dragon swooped under him. Angel grabbed the edge of a wing membrane, felt the thin tissue tear, and heard the dragon bellow in pain.

The beast stayed under him. Sharp scales sliced through Angel's shirt, into his flesh. Light flashed and shimmered...and then he was on the ground.

Angel held a hand to the wound in his shoulder, staggered to his feet and swayed in shock and pain.

The dragon shrugged his shoulders, shaking the upper part of his body like a dog shaking off water. His long neck snaked out until his eyes were level with Angel's. His great horned head wove back and forth, snakelike, but the hot breath streaming from his nostrils was as sweet as burnt sugar.

When the fanged mouth, nearly a foot across, neared the slash in Angel's skin, the dragon blew gently. Warm air rushed across Angel. The pain faded...disappeared. Twisting his shoulder in wonder, Angel looked back into the great turquoise eyes regarding him so steadily. An image drifted into his mind.

A girl, not more than eighteen struggles determinedly across the hot desert rocks. Her eyes are ringed with exhaustion and her feet shuffle like someone on the verge of fainting. She is watched by deep blue eyes.

Shocked, Angel watched the vision unfolding before him. He knows that girl...

"Mom?" he whispers...

The girl staggers through the cleft in the rocks, down the stony trail and with a low cry, stumbles toward the spring hidden in the ravine. Before she can drink, she falls unconscious. The watching dragon shimmers, then an Anasazi warrior steps into the sun and kneels beside her. He dribbles water into her mouth; his hand passes over her brow and her eyes flutter open.

"I am Nah-chu-ru," he says. "Don't be afraid."

She smiles. "I ain't. I ain't at all...You got the bluest eyes, I ever seen..."

The image faded. Angel sighed and looked into his father's eyes. The dragon shape shimmered and the Anasazi warrior stood before him, his hands held out.

Across the dust, Gary's truck backfired again.

"Celsa!" Angel turned and ran toward the caves. Behind him, he heard the whoosh of great wings beating their way into the sky.

EIGHTEEN

The dust cloud kicked up by Gary's truck churned closer. Angel sprinted toward the cave ledge. He had to get the backpack out of sight, and fast. If Gary caught them...

He clambered up the rock face, grabbed the pack and slid into shadow.

"Celsa!" He shook her shoulder.

"Angel...Lemme sleep..."

"Wake up!" he hissed. "It's Gary. He's heading this way!"

That brought her wide awake. She sat up quickly, banging her head into Angel's chin.

"Ow!" The pain was a relief – it distracted him from the pictures haunting his thoughts.

"Has he seen us?" Celsa demanded. "If anyone finds us, Hydemann will make sure we never get back here again. This is our only chance."

"If Gary finds us here," Angel whispered, "we might not even make it out."

"No," Celsa argued. "He wouldn't..." Her voice trailed off when she saw the look in Angel's eyes. "So they got us coming and going. *Hay-ya-yay!* How close is he?"

Angel dropped to his stomach and crawled to the lip of the cave. The dust cloud was closer – a lot closer.

"Maybe a mile," he whispered. "He's moving fast."

Celsa slid down beside him. "Should we run for it?

Angel shook his head. "He's got the truck. And he can run really fast – he'd catch us for sure."

"I hope he doesn't look this way, then," Celsa said. They lay flat, feeling the seconds crawl by. The rumbling motor seemed to roll over and over the landscape. Before long, Angel could see Gary's silhouette behind the wheel.

"He's got a turquoise dig going around here," Angel whispered. "I think it has to be at the sacred mountain."

Celsa turned to him. "Is he crazy?"

Angel nodded, smiling a little. "Yeah, he sure is."

Celsa snorted. "Then, we'd better be awfully careful. I'll bet *señor* Hydemann finds out quick because, I hope you don't mind me saying so, but I think your father's too stupid to keep his own secrets."

"He's not my father!"

"Shh!"

Angel looked away, raging inside, and then the weirdness made him laugh softly. His real dad was a giant lizard, and as far as he was concerned, that was still a whole lot better than Gary.

The truck came on and on, then without warning, swerved to follow a track that was invisible to them. Ahead of the vehicle, storm clouds were sheeting rain on the flanks of the sacred mountain. In a moment, the truck was swallowed by the haze. The two sat up and stared after it.

"We'd better keep going," Celsa said wearily. "We're too visible here. And we don't know how long before he'll come back."

Angel nodded and shrugged on his backpack. "We can't go across the flatlands," he said.

"I know," Celsa agreed.

Once down from the ledge, they veered away from the easy incline leading to the mountain, turning instead toward the rough tumbles of rocks and foothills that led spinelike to the southern slope.

Stands of pinon trees and cottonwoods shaded the arroyos in some places. When they could, they trudged between the trunks or when the way got too rough, between weathered spires of rock. They tried to avoid the arroyos – the dry streambeds weren't dry now. Most gurgled with muddy, brown water. When they had to cross one, Celsa and Angel stood motionless, craning their necks to look upstream, listening for the dull thunder of an approaching flash flood. When they were sure they heard nothing, they tore through even the smallest streams, splashing, slipping and scrambling up the far bank to higher ground.

The trail looked more and more familiar to Angel. He felt the tug of the other boy's memories...the calls of his clan. He pushed them away and kept walking.

The heat mounted. Their progress was slow, and both of them were covered in scrapes and bruises, the result of missed footing and jabbing desert plants.

Two rocks rose up ahead. "This way," Angel said. "There's water and shade that way."

"How do you know?" Celsa demanded. "Did you hold out on me? Have you been here before?"

"No. I just know," he said wearily.

Her eyes bored into his, but he turned away.

We are walking into the valley of the dragons, he thinks – and he knows it's true.

The way is more difficult than his memory tells him. Recklessly, Angel laughs. Whose memory is it? His mother's? The boy he has dreamt about so many times? His father – the dragon? Angel shut that thought away. He couldn't deal with it.

As he and Celsa wound their way through the pillars of rock and scrambled over heaps of stone, he felt the familiar strength beginning to hum in his skin and muscles.

"No!" he cried.

"No what?" Celsa demanded. Her face was grimed with dust and she swayed with fatigue. Her eyes squinted. "You're glowing again, Angel."

He dropped to his knees, clenching his fists and pressing them against his belly. He wouldn't give in. He wouldn't be like one of those freaky characters in the movies who kept morphing into different creatures. He wouldn't let go of himself.

Celsa crouched beside him, holding a water bottle to his lips.

"Don't let me change,' he gasped. "Keep me here!"

She gripped his hand so hard it hurt. Waves of images, sounds and scents bombarded his mind.

"*Esta bien.* You aren't going anywhere," she said. "I won't let go, Angel." Tightening her grasp even more, she caught a fistful of his shirt. She leaned over him as though her solid weight would anchor him to the earth.

Angel felt them...felt them all. The dragons drew near and nearer. They would be invisible to human eyes – all shimmering desert light and rocky shadows. They would swirl in the wind storms and their fire would strike like lightning across the land.

"My son," a voice whispered in his mind. *"It is I, Nah-chu-ru, your father who calls you!"*

"We have waited, Angel," the voice of the grandfather spoke to him. *"It is time to come to your people..."*

"You're not my people!" Angel screamed. "Stop it! Stop it!"

The voices stopped abruptly. The feeling of otherness disappeared. Angel gasped and ground his fist into his eye. "It's okay now," he said to Celsa. She didn't move. "It's okay," he repeated. "They're gone."

She let go slowly, straightening stiffly as if her muscles had hardened like the rocks. "You sure?"

"Yeah." He sat back and scrubbed at his face again. Celsa watched, her face tight.

"What happened," she asked. .

"I...I..." Angel stumbled for words. He sat back on the dirt and clutched his knees.

"Tell me what's going on." Her voice was thin, strained. "I felt something...people... ghosts...all around us. And you were glowing again. What's happening, Angel?"

He shouldn't tell her, he thought dully. She'd think he'd gone crazy just like his mom. But he had to talk about it with someone – and there wasn't anyone else.

"Okay," his voice was husky. "But it's really, really weird."

"I'm listening." She sat down in front of him, clasping her knees. Her eyes focused on his face and her expression only flickered slightly as he slowly began to tell her how the crazy magic had started with flashes of anger, built to waking dreams, and then grown to these mind-numbing changes. Celsa listened in complete silence, watching his eyes. As Angel finished telling her about his last transformation – about his *father* – he realized that despite the afternoon heat, he was shivering.

"...so my mother wasn't crazy. My father is a blue desert spirit. Just what every kid wants." His voice reverberated with bitterness.

He waited for Celsa to say something, but she sunk her chin on her knees and stared at the ground.

"You...you don't have to be scared of me or anything" he said.

She raised her eyes then. "I'm not," she said. *"Oye!* I've never heard anything like this...but it makes sense."

"Are you crazy? How can it makes sense!"

Celsa shrugged. "I was thinking about *señor* Hydemann – how he's a nice man mostly, but he's just *loco* about anyone trespassing on his land. He chases them off, sends them to jail – there isn't anything he won't do to trespassers. I'll bet he knows all about these dragons, or spirits or whatever, and that's why he keeps everyone out."

"That's stupid..." Angel shot back, furious.

"Why?" Celsa demanded. "Why would it be stupid for him to know about the dragons, Angel? His family has owned this land for five generations – more than a hundred years. I think you should talk to him. I bet he can help you – and your mom, too."

"No! I don't want any help from him!" Angel yelled. "You don't get it!"

"I'm trying to." Celsa reached out and gripped his hand. He yanked it back and leapt up, wiping his arm across his eyes. He should be happy that he wasn't crazy. But he felt stupid – and just as scared.

Celsa watched him silently. "You want to make camp here," she asked, "or go farther?"

"Any place is better than here," Angel snapped.

"Whatever – but we'd better stay under cover. Who knows what Gary's doing. And for sure, *señor* Hydemann will be following. No matter what he knows, he won't be happy about us being out here."

Celsa's practical voice sent a chill down Angel's spine. Could the man know about the dragons? About his mother? About *him?* Unable and unwilling to explain this tangle of emotions to Celsa, Angel nodded curtly and shouldered his pack. He let her lead the way, too exhausted and keyed up to care.

All around him he heard rustling whispers, saw flashes of light, caught whiffs of smoky sweet smells. The dragons were all there, just beyond the edge of his sight. As they traveled, Angel felt their great eyes watching. Celsa didn't seem to notice anything as she marched stoically ahead. The late afternoon sun cast long shadows and draped the rocky cliffs in purple and blue.

The way between the rock walls wound down to a deep, green canyon. Once Celsa stopped and pointed upward. The slightly squared caves in the rocks above showed they had once been inhabited by people.

"Anasazi probably." Celsa's voice held longing. "No one else knows they're here. They're probably full of artifacts – gold, silver, turquoise, pottery..." her voice trailed away.

"Hydemann probably knows," Angel said.

"Yeah, probably." Celsa sighed, readjusted her pack and set out again.

An eagle screamed above them, but there were no other sounds.

"We can't get up there without a ladder," she said as they hiked below the rows of caves. "I'll bet there are finds there. Maybe wall paintings. Maybe Hydemann never looked himself – just kept people away. If we had a ladder..."

"We don't," Angel snapped. "Keep going. We have a long way to go."

Celsa rolled her eyes, but said nothing. As they passed around the jutting edge of the cliff, Angel wondered if the path and stairs cut into the rock wall were still there. This was the way to his Grandfather's kiva. This was the place where his ancestors had died.

He kept his head down and followed Celsa.

NINETEEN

They walked until the creeping darkness made it too hard to see. Angel heard the dragon voices wistfully calling him. He shut his mind to them. He would not, *would not* turn into something he didn't want to be. He would not give in and lose himself like his mother had.

"We've got to stop," Celsa said at last.

Angel shrugged. "Whatever."

"There's a spot over there, I think." She pointed to a sheltered hollow against the rock face. Angel would have liked to put miles between him and the kiva, but Celsa had stumbled repeatedly as the twilight deepened. She had to rest.

They climbed wearily over the stones that blocked their way and looked around. This place would do. A rock slab leaning against the cliff face formed a stony lean-to. If the rumbling clouds dumped rain they would be protected. Angel wondered if there would be flash floods in the canyon.

With a sigh, Celsa laid down her pack, opened it and dug for their food. She popped opened two cans of stew and handed one to Angel. As they scooped the sticky mush from the can with their dirty fingers, she sometimes glanced at him from under her lashes. Angel ate slowly, leaning almost motionless against the rock, all his energy sapped by the continual fight against the whispers snaking through his mind.

"Y'okay?" Celsa asked once.

"What?"

"Are you okay?" she repeated.

The voices pressed over her words. Angel fought back with a wall of images – the motel, school, his mother. "They're trying to get me. In my mind."

She crawled over beside him. "We should turn back – get you away from here, Angel."

He didn't answer, almost unaware of her now. She watched him uncertainly, seeing the blue light glowing and fading around his body.

Angel sat perfectly still. Fighting. Waiting.

They were so alive, so wild….He could hardly resist them now…. His eyes drifted shut and he stood again in the smoky kiva. *The bodies of his people encircle him. There is silence and sadness.*

The grandfather speaks. "We are of one clan, the people and the great serpent Tieholtsodi. Your wandering has been long and our sadness has been great. Come back to your people, Angel."

For the first time, Angel speaks. "People of the sky…why do you hunt me? Please don't make me… don't catch me in a net I can't escape from…"

"There is no net. There is no danger. We are your people."

The chanting in the room fills Angel's mind and heart. It holds a rhythm and words he knows. He is ready to dance the great dances in the kivas…he sways to the beating drum…a mother scoops her child into the pattern of the dance…

His mother!

"No!" Angel leapt to his feet, knocking into Celsa. She grabbed his arm, steadying him.

"Angel!"

He turned to her slowly, eyes refocusing on her square face. With a surge of emotion, he realized how grateful he was to not be alone. He wished he hadn't left her before.

"You gotta sleep, Angel," Celsa urged him.

He shook his head. "Not yet." Then he realized his mind had quieted – that the dragon voices were gone. Without thinking, he stroked his amulet, missing the warm companionship of the kiva. He sighed.

Celsa was sitting up, propped against a wall, but her head kept bobbing down and her eyes drifted closed. "Y'okay?" she said drowsily. She yawned, still clutching his arm. Gently, he uncurled her fingers from his sleeve. Angel laughed.

She jerked upright. "What?"

"You were asleep."

"No, I wasn't."

"Lie down. You won't be able to keep going tomorrow if you don't sleep."

"I'm okay." She yawned again. "What about you?"

"No worries. They…they're gone, for now." He tried to keep his voice even and sure.

She nodded. "*Bien*. If they come back…if it starts…wake me up, okay?" She slid down and curled into a ball. Within seconds her breathing stretched into long, slow rhythms.

With a sigh, Angel stretched out with his pack under his head. He stared up at the stars. He didn't feel himself glide into sleep.

The long days and nights blend into each other – a time of hunger, despair, heat and cold. The boy waits for death. It is the only way he knows to rejoin his people. He travels many miles, running, walking, and then stumbling. At last, he falls unconscious.

The girl, daughter of the Navaho, finds him there. From her bag, she dribbles water into his parched lips, shades him with her body, and waves the flies away with her hands. Even when darkness deepens over the land, she does not leave him.

The hard light of the full moon falls across his face and his eyes flutter open. He gasps, thinking the daughter of Tieholtsodi has come. Then he sees that even though this girl is beautiful, she does not carry magic in her being.

He closes his eyes in shame. He has allowed his people to die and only death awaits him.

The scream of a mountain lion pierces his ears. The girl presses close to him, so close he feels her shivering. The puma pads closer and closer.

"Let me die, brother," he whispers to the cat.

"I don't want to die," the girl hisses. "Wake up, warrior. Help me!"

His eyes open again. He does not care if he dies, but no one else should die because of his weakness.

Slowly the young man gets to his feet. He wavers with exhaustion, but he grips his atlatl and faces the great cat. The moonlight gleams in the animal's eyes and shimmers on its fur as it leaps. The boy cries out as claws rake his shoulder, ripping muscle and tendon, but somehow he holds his spear steady. Howling, the mountain lion writhes on the spear, shattering it. The animal drops heavily to the packed earth. The light fades from its eyes.

The girl leads the boy back to her people. He stands before their hogans with tears washing down his chest. His atlatl is gone; his people are gone; he has nothing left but his flute. The weight of wounds and despair press on him until he knows he will never walk straight again...

Angel muttered and rolled in his dreams.

He is the flute player now, wandering between the tribes, north, south, east and west. All are the same to him. He has left his wife and baby behind – they are happy in the arms of their family and friends. He alone thinks of his brothers and sisters, his aunts and uncles, of the grandfather he betrayed.

Someday, he whispers to the night stars, someday I will fly through the night and find you. He wonders if the daughter of Tieholtsodi has returned to the third world, or if she lives among another people. He wonders if she has found a husband who is worthy of her.

He sits on a great rock, staring at the night sky and distant dawn, and sends his flute song across the desert and years. In a distant hogan, his young son lifts his head from the spear he is polishing; he listens and takes the song of Kokopeli into his heart...

TWENTY

When the sun seeped liquid gold over the purple hills, Angel and Celsa were already preparing to move on. The sacred mountain looked closer this morning, great and beckoning, rising above the shelf of grey clouds.

Angel felt the dragons everywhere, saw them swooping in crystalline flashes against the sky. But the voices in his head were gone. He could have laughed aloud with joy, both at their beauty and at his own sense of freedom. He was himself again.

Almost himself. As he stuffed the remains of their scant breakfast into his pack, he sized up Celsa. If he was newly charged with life – strong as a yellow-blooming chamisa, she was like a cholla that had endured too long a drought. Her face had dulled to a grey-tan; smoky smudges blurred the snap in her eyes.

"Once we get to the mountain, we can hide out – rest as long as we need to," Angel said, measuring the distance through narrowed eyes. "I bet we can get to there by noon,"

Celsa licked her cracked lips. "Depends on the path. It took us forever to go not so far yesterday."

"Today will be different," Angel replied.

She laughed, a thin wisp compared to her old belly laugh. "Whatever you say."

They set out slowly at first, Celsa trudging with clenched teeth. Angel led the way, picking his way through the cracked stones and crumbling trenches. As the sun warmed the morning, Celsa's stiff movements eased and she didn't complain when he picked up the pace.

This back path toward the sacred mountain wound through ragged canyons topped with brush and stubby trees, threading between spires of weathered rock like the falling walls of an ancient city. The landscape camouflaged their passing. But at last, the hidden ways ran out. Around eleven o'clock Celsa and Angel crouched in the shade of a thick juniper and stared across the barren mesa. Open ground for about three miles, broken only by an occasional cactus or juniper. No cover worth speaking of. His emerald green back pack and Celsa's red shirt would be visible for miles.

Celsa sucked down the last of the water in her canteen and sighed. "Okay," she said. "Let's go."

Angel hesitated. "We could wait until night."

She shook her head. "I'm too tired. If I don't step on something poisonous, I'll fall into a ravine in the dark."

They took advantage of what cover they could, but there wasn't much to be had. The dust devils whirled excitedly around them. Angel's eyes could make out the flashing silver and turquoise of many small dragons within the twisting air. They chittered excitedly, but without much sense. Above, the greater dragons, his father among them, soared against the sky. Around the mountain, thick clouds were building again, grey-green waves rolling ominously across the sky.

At the edge of a dry wash, Celsa squinted at the rumbling thunderheads. "*Oye!* We may not be worrying about running out of water."

Angel nodded. "We'd better stay on high ground."

They veered slightly to their right away from a network of small arroyos, toward a stretch of land slightly higher than that around it.

Even Angel was sweating profusely as they scrambled over a patch of crumbled stone. As he reached back to give Celsa a hand, lightning flashes ricocheted in their eyes. Thunder cracked and rolled across the land. Hot air suddenly blasted across the mesa, bending the junipers sideways and spraying dust into their faces. Scrunching shut their eyes and mouths, holding hands over their noses, they leaned into the wind.

"Here it comes," Celsa yelled.

The rain sheeted across the mesa like a tsunami. Drops drove like bullets onto their heads and puffed against the ground. More and more. Faster and harder. Wind whipped their clothes; rain pummeled their faces. Angel wrapped his arms around Celsa; they leaned their heads together, gasping for dry air, holding down their hats, protecting their faces.

Water pooled and gushed at their feet, streaming over ground that was too dry and packed to absorb it. Pebbles rattled as the drops exploded into puddles and rolled into thousands of rivulets.

Lightning struck again and again. Their eyelids pulsated with red flashes. *Crack!* A juniper exploded only yards away.

"*Hay-ya-yay!* We have to get out of this," Celsa gasped. "The lightning will get us!"

"Take my hand," Angel shouted. "We have to keep hold of each other."

They tried to run, but water poured from the brims of their hats, half-blinding them. Their mud caked jeans stiffened like wet plaster on their legs. The wind gusted around them like a monster licking its lips.

Beneath their feet, the ground oozed mud, sticking and sucking as they ran and stumbled. And then, as they battled their way across the land, Angel heard a sound that whined and rose against the noise of the storm – the growling of a straining engine.

Gasping, he tried to peer through the rain. A few hundred yards away, a flash of light tilted up from the ground. Headlights. The truck's motor roared again.

"Celsa! A truck!" Angel shouted. "It's stuck on the trail."

They stopped, eyes searching through the downpour. A flash of lightning briefly illuminated the landscape.

"It's white," she yelled. "Hydemann!"

Angel looked around wildly. They had to get away before the truck broke free of the mud, before the rancher spotted them

"We've got to go faster!" He yanked Celsa's hand.

They ran again, forcing their exhausted muscles to push out more and more energy. Angel felt the hum of dragon strength in his veins but resolutely blocked it. That wouldn't help Celsa.

The ground beneath them rose. The sacred mountain loomed above.

Muddy water cascaded between rocks and brush. The footing was treacherous – a wrong step would send them crashing down onto loose stones, maybe causing a landslide to gather and crush them.

Angel's eyes searched upward, looking for the path he remembered from his dreams. *His feet had walked this path...*

"This way!" He pulled Celsa along a rim of rock, then stopped. Yes, ahead, less than ten yards stood the boulder that hid the path the people had taken to the sacred place. A glimmer of memory fired through Angel's mind. A memory of a dusty path leading to the great cave that shone with turquoise light. It was this way – beyond that rock, a few clambering steps and they would be on the secret path – safe from Hydemann; safe from Gary.

Except...between them and the path roared a torrent of foaming brown water.

There had been no storms, no floods in his dream memory. Angel shifted from foot to foot. He could see the familiar rocks, the steps they made toward the mountain. He knew how they would feel under his feet, but could they get there?

Celsa's breath came hard beside him. She wiped her face with her arm, leaving a streak of mud. "Is that the way?"

"Yeah. It's the path up the mountain – to the sacred place. But we have to get across the water."

She nodded, too exhausted by the hours of fighting through the land and weather to question his statement. "Can we wade through it?"

Behind them they heard the rumble of a truck. Hydemann had cleared the mudhole.

"We have to," Angel said through gritted teeth.

They plunged in. Immediately the water surged up to their knees. Celsa lost her footing and nearly went down, but Angel clung to her arm, hauling her to her feet.

Step by step, they inched their way through the mud brown flood. They felt their way with their feet, probing with toes to find solid footing.

"Ow!" A rock, carried by the flood, smashed against Angel's leg. He lurched, almost buckled, but Celsa held on to him.

One foot...another...slipping...steady...steady...plunging into a hole...nearly losing balance...wet...everything muddy and wet...step...another...

Angel scrambled up the bank, his clothes and skin oozing mud. Hardly able to see for the wet and grime, he dragged Celsa behind him. They dug their fingers into slick mud, jamming them against embedded stones. The torrent sucked at their legs. They inched above the water and lay on the ground, gasping.

Behind, the growling motor chased them like a nightmare monster.

"Come on!" Angel cried. He pulled Celsa up and they scrambled, slipping and crawling, to crouch behind the boulder as Hydemann's truck plowed slowly up the streambed. The water churned away from the wheels. Even on its high carriage, the engine bounced only inches above the waterline.

Shivering, Angel and Celsa kneeled behind the boulder watching the truck make its slow way up the mountainside.

"There must be a road or wide trail up there," Celsa said, "or Hydemann wouldn't have risked the flood."

Angel searched his memory; he saw it again – the place where the people gathered before entering their sacred place. "Yeah, there is. The flood is running over a trail that widens out onto a big flat area."

"So why are Gary and Hydemann going there?" Celsa demanded. "What's up there, Angel?" Her eyes searched his face.

"A cave," he said. "Old...real old...full of turquoise."

"How do you know that?"

"I know," Angel said. "I just know."

Celsa thrust her face closer. "Explain – or did you hold out on me again, *partner!*"

Angel shook his head. "No! I...I'm getting their memories. They're playing through my mind like I was there, like I was a different person. He was in the caves and I remember it like it was me. But it wasn't me. It wasn't ever me. I know it sounds weird, but you have to believe me. You have to...I'm not lying...it's weird for me, too." He trailed off.

Celsa eyed him a moment longer, then nodded her head curtly.

Angel let out a long breath and peered ahead trying to spot either truck. If Gary had found the sacred cave, had *dirtied* it with his greed...

When the sound of the motor was lost in gusting wind, Angel stood up.

Celsa wearily got to her feet. "Is it much farther?"

Angel shook his head. "No. The cave's maybe another mile. But we don't know that's where Gary's mining – or where Hydemann's looking for him."

"I don't care where they are," Celsa snapped. "I just want to get out of this rain, get our treasure – whatever it is – and get out of here without being seen."

Angel led the way, his footing sure. He remembered it all – the twists and turns in the path, the crack in the rock that led to the center of the sacred mountain. He could see in his mind the first cave where seams of turquoise had shone like streaks of sky in his people's torchlight. Beyond that, well hidden waited yet another cavern. There the turquoise rose in thick, ropey columns, the cool blue laced with black lines. And then, there was the last cavern – a place where the turquoise was so rich, so elegantly carved by the artists of his people, that the chamber seemed to glow in blues and greens of underwater light. In the center of that cavern, a deep, silent pool marked the path to the other worlds. As memory after memory crowded through his tired thoughts, Angel ached to be there again.

An hour later, he and Celsa eased cautiously around a jutting bluff. Before them, the ground spread out, flat and fan-shaped. Several hundred people could have camped there. The creek that was now the roaring flood would have provided water. The gathering ground seemed to butt against a weathered cliff that was crenellated with pockets and cracks. But Angel remembered that one crack was the entrance. He would have missed it if he hadn't already known it was there.

But Gary had not missed it. Tire tracks scarred the earth. The old red truck was backed in almost to the crack – easier to load the turquoise, Angel thought bitterly. And not far from that, parked closer to the water, Hydemann's truck shone sullenly in the half light. With a flare of rage, Angel straightened, clenching his fists. Old songs thrummed in his mind. His fingers curled as if to hold an atlatl, ready to fight his people's enemies.

"Careful!" Celsa dragged him back, shattering his mood.

Angel leaned against the rock, breathing hard.

"You're glowing again," Celsa told him. "You're giving off so much light, we won't even need a flashlight. We were *loco* to do this," she muttered, trying to wring water from her braids. She crammed the hat back over the sodden tangles.

Angel turned his head to study the cave entrance. "Gary and Hydemann shouldn't be here," he said. "This is a sacred place. I've got to stop them – chase them away from here."

"Yeah, sure thing, blue boy. I'll just call our troops," Celsa said. "Oh wait, I forgot – we don't have any."

The wind gusted by, bringing another spray of cold rain. She swore and sagged against the cold stone.

Angel ignored her. A fierce anger was growing on him. Gary, in this place! It was wrong that he was strutting through the sacred halls. He wouldn't know about Tieholtsodi or her people. He wouldn't admire the artistry of the stone carved centuries ago. He wouldn't pause to read their history. He wouldn't care, not about the magic, the beauty, or the old lives. All Gary would care about was hacking away chunks of turquoise.

And what about Hydemann? Why was he here? Had he known about the ancient treasures, or had he simply tracked Gary across the mesas? Was he a protector or another greedy thief?

Angel flexed his arms. Dragon strength flashed in his veins, but it wasn't capturing him into an alien life. It was merging with him. He, Angel, who was on a mission to save his mother, and he, Angel, the son of a great dragon could come together. The threads of all their pasts would merge in this place. All his people and their treasures would be protected.

TWENTY-ONE

Angel heard the whispers of the dragons as he strode toward the entrance to the cave. He also heard Celsa...

"What are you *doing!*" she shouted. "Are you crazy?"

Angel shook off her hand. "You've seen that I'm changing. Maybe this is why. This is a sacred place – a *magic* place. Gary will wreck it, just to get some turquoise. And what will Hydemann do – add to his bank account? I can't let that happen. This is the door between the worlds – the place of the dragons."

"Then let the dragons deal with him," Celsa snapped, hauling on his shirt. "If Gary or Hydemann catch us, we're in trouble. *Mas problemas.* The kind that doesn't go away – you know that. We can hide, and when they leave, we'll find our treasure."

Angel hesitated. *Treasure.* He had forgotten about the treasure, and that meant he had forgotten about his mom. A wave of shame washed over him. He was like the boy who had forgotten his people...but were these ghost dragons his people now?

A crack like thunder rumbled from the cave entrance.

"That was a gun shot." Celsa's voice quivered.

They stared at the cave entrance, frozen. A moment later, Gary tore from the shadows, his shotgun hanging loosely from his hand. He ran, slipping slightly on the slick ground until he got to Hydemann's truck. Yanking open the door, he jumped in. The motor roared to life.

"What's he doing?" Celsa hissed.

"I dunno."

They watched as the man cranked the wheel of the truck, turning it around so that the hood faced the roaring water. The stream that Celsa and Angel had managed to ford had risen wildly in the past hour as water rushed down from the mountain. Gary got out of the truck – the motor rumbled above the crashing of wind and water. Gun in hand, he stood back as the truck, still in gear, rolled slowly toward the flood. When the wheels stalled on a rock, Gary got behind the vehicle and shoved. It bounced, churned mud, and then careened over the bank into the torrent. The truck swung sideways, smashed against rocks, and then lazily spun round and round. The open door tore off, disappearing into the surge of floodwater.

From behind the boulder, Angel and Celsa watched open-mouthed as the vehicle rolled, twisted and bounced downstream. Within minutes, it was out of sight.

Celsa hauled Angel down into a tight crouch behind the rocks. "We can't take chances – can't let Gary see us," she hissed. Her eyes were wide, pupils black. "He must have...must have..." her voice faltered.

Angel swallowed. "He shot Hydemann."

Celsa clutched his arm with both fists, as though she was having trouble keeping her balance. "We have to get help. We can...we can steal the truck."

Angel chewed his lip, forcing his tumbling mind to focus. "How? What if there are no keys? And we'd never make it across the flood. It's too high. We have to stay here – stay hidden – until Gary leaves."

Celsa nodded and for a moment they stayed silent, shoulder to shoulder, trying to ignore their shivering. Then Celsa nudged him. "Gary can't leave either. Not with the flood and all." She looked up at the dull sky. "We may all be spending the night here."

When Angel didn't answer, she sighed, unfastened her pack and dug out a mashed packet of food. Unwrapping it, she offered some to Angel. When he ignored it, she sighed again and without trying to protect the food from the rain, began scooping the mess into her mouth.

Angel was barely aware of her as the dragon voices swelled into his mind. Urgent. Angry. Caught in exhaustion and horror, he was past pushing them away or even knowing what they were trying to tell him.

"Angel, what if Gary didn't kill *señor* Hydemann?" Celsa's words barely registered over the squawks, whistles and cries that arrowed into his consciousness. He dragged his mind over to Celsa – to the reality he knew.

"That...that'd be good."

"Angel," her fingers tightened on his wet sleeve, "what if *señor* Hydemann's in there hurt...bleeding? What if he isn't dead? What if he's hiding? What if he's bleeding and dying slow?"

The dragons howled. Angel's heart throbbed. "I thought you didn't like him. You said he's the rich man – and your papa and mama stay poor working for him."

Celsa's eyes filled. "He's been good to my family. I just get mad because he's got so much and *mi mamá y papá* work so hard. But he works hard too – and…and he's helping pay for Jenny's tuition…." Celsa clutched his arm. "He's a good man, Angel. What're we going to do?"

The bodies of his people lie on the ground…their skin grey in death. The boy cries out…

The voices of the dragons filled his mind, but he couldn't make sense of them…not with the terror…the grief…He couldn't stand it. He had to do something.

"I'll go in and look," Angel said. "I know the way. Maybe I can make myself have some dragon strength." He stood up slowly, stiffly, willing dragon strength to blaze through his blood. "Wait here for me. If I don't come out, go for help as soon as the river goes down."

"No," Celsa said gripping the rock to boost herself to her feet.

"What do you mean, no? I have to go."

"*Sí*. And I'm going too. Do you think I'm going to stay out here and be safe when the man that helped my family might be in there dying?"

Angel grabbed her. "Gary's in there and he's crazy – desperate! It isn't safe!"

"I don't want to talk any more," Celsa snapped. Her voice shook only a little. "Lead on, blue boy."

Too weary to argue, Angel shrugged. Leaving their packs hidden behind the boulder, they moved forward slowly, hugging the rock face. At the crack that split the cliff, they pressed against the rock, listening. Nothing.

"If you can get that glowing thing going again," Celsa whispered, "now's a good time. I left my flashlight in the pack."

"I'll do my best."

Angel led the way. The cool walls leaned close, like great hands of rock with palms pressed in prayer, masking that this was an entrance to a much larger cave. Compared to the howling wind outside, it was quiet with every sound melting into a muffled echo. The air was cool, but dry. Angel laid his own palms against the rock, feeling the prayers of thousands of years.

"Yes, my son...yes."

The dragons, his people, swelled into his willing awareness; the cacophony of minds no longer clutched at his thoughts. Clearly, he saw each one, each ancestor standing behind him, pouring energy into him. His blood sang with their strength; his mind throbbed with their fierce passions.

"You're glowing," Celsa whispered. Angel heard a half-hysterical giggle in her voice.

"Yes," he whispered.

They edged forward the mouth of the first cavern. A battery powered light shone on one rock face, but its thin light was enough to illuminate the cave. Stalagmites rose high toward a roof studded with crystalline rocks that shone star-like amid the streaking blue of turquoise. The walls waved with wide veins of the gemstone. Angel's eyes traveled down to the wall where the full light of the lantern pointed. A vein of turquoise had been gouged and hacked, large chunks piled to one side, and splinters scattered carelessly over the floor.

Angel felt a growl rising in his chest. Ancient anger pulsed through his muscles.

"Tone it down!" Celsa whispered. "We don't need a floodlight."

Angel's senses were sharpening. His ears picked up the music of rushing water and sighing drafts. He tasted the cool, wet air that drifted by them. The tang of turquoise floated in the breeze...turquoise and blood!

The growl rose in his chest again. Forgetting caution, he strode out across the cave, following the scent. He saw the shadows of his small brothers and sisters flitting high above, keening anxiously. *The magic stick that had hurt the man could hurt them too...the enemy man has found the sacred cave...the enemy...*

Angel's muscles remember the slow, crouching pace of the hunter. His atlatl is gone – he has nothing to fight the enemy with but his courage, cunning, and growing strength.

A footfall scrapes in the distance...Gary has entered the next cavern – the cave of ceremony, where so long ago the boy had been cleansed before his journey to the third world. He failed his people then...he will not fail them now. His own feet begin the dance of the hunter.

"My son..." whispers his father.

"Your family greets you..." says the grandfather.

Crack! Angel cried out and clutched his arm. Celsa, still holding the rock she has slammed him with, stood in front of him, panting.

"Blue, I can take," she hissed. "But you can't go out of your mind too."

Grunting his fury, Angel tried to push by her.

"Are we partners?" Celsa's voice seemed like splintering rocks in his divided mind.

He smelled the blood on the air, heard Gary's almost silent footsteps. He grabbed Celsa, shoved her into shadow, clamping his hand over her mouth. She bit down hard, but he didn't let go. Then she stiffened, listening, and stopped fighting him.

A flashlight bobbed over the walls briefly as Gary hurried into the cavern. He went to the mining lantern, dropped the flashlight and grabbed the larger light. Near running, he headed back to where he had come.

"Let's go," Angel whispered. "Hydemann's in the next cavern. I...I can taste his blood in the air."

Celsa's breath went into her, in a sharp little gasp, but she stood up, the rock held in her fist. "Then let's go get him!"

TWENTY-TWO

Lit by his soft blue glow, Angel and Celsa moved quickly toward the dark corner of the cavern where the passage to the next cave was hidden in shadow. After one sharp bend, the passage straightened and broadened, the sides and floor smoothed out eons ago by Angel's ancestors. He went ahead of Celsa. He could hear the slow flap of wings high above the floor ahead.

"Is the man Hydemann dead, my father?" Angel probed outward with his mind.

"No...not yet...but soon...he bleeds..."

"What must I do to save him?"

"We will not let him die," says the grandfather, *"but the enemy can kill us with his magic stick. We can heal the man's wounds, but not our own."*

"The enemy is here!" Rage sharpens the thoughts flung out by his father. *"He destroys the sacred place. Can you fight like a warrior?*

"No...but I'll think of something."

Angel stepped back, and touched Celsa. "You were right," he whispered in her ear so the sound would not carry. "Hydemann's wounded in the next cavern."

She hefted her rock. "My aim's not bad. I can nail Gary."

"Don't be stupid," Angel hissed. "Then he'll know we're here and take his time shooting us."

"Okay, then what's your plan, O mighty blue one?"

Ignoring her sarcasm, Angel took a deep, steadying breath. "I think Hydemann's near the entrance of the next cave, wounded...probably bleeding. I'm going to distract Gary while you try to get Hydemann back to the first cave. I think...I think the dragons will help him. They'll keep him from dying."

"Fantastic," Celsa snapped. "And who's going to keep you from dying?"

"No one," Angel said. "He's my foster father. He won't hurt me."

"Are you *loco*? He'll shoot you and throw you in the river." Celsa punched Angel's already sore arm for emphasis.

Angel looked at her helplessly. He knew that. But another plan was forming in his mind...one that he didn't really want anyone to know about. *He* didn't even want to know about it. Celsa's face moved in close to his.

"What are you really going to do?"

Angel licked his lips. He could taste death on the air. The dragons' thoughts in his mind and wingbeats high above his head became more frantic.

"Celsa, don't waste time. Save Hydemann!" He turned back toward the Cavern of Ceremonies.

As his dragon senses sharpened, Angel could see through the shadows to the magnificence that rose on all sides. Blue and green wound together in rich colors and carvings, a work of art that spanned a thousand years.

In the center of the cavern, a small cold stream gurgled across the floor, widening between the turquoise studded columns into a clear, dark pool. The boy had been cleansed there. Angel remembered it as clearly as though the blue sands had scrubbed his own skin.

Gary was standing by one of the great carved pillars, pickaxe swung back, ready to hack the treasure into saleable chunks. To his right, Angel felt death flowing toward the wounded rancher. Above, the dragons whirred and keened at pitches too high for human ears.

Before he could panic and run, Angel strode across the rock floor toward the beam highlighting his foster father. "Hey Gary!" he called. "Need some help?"

Cursing, Gary swung around, lowering his pickaxe. With a loud clatter, he dropped it, groped for his gun and with the other hand picked up the lantern. Swinging the beam toward Angel, he cocked his gun in a swift motion.

Behind him, Angel heard the soft sounds of Celsa sliding in the dark toward the rancher. Keeping his eyes on his foster father, Angel moved forward as though this was the motel office and he was offering to clean the rooms.

"What the...! What are you doing here?" Gary snarled.

"Just looking around," Angel said. "I saw your truck. Hey, Gary, let me help. Let me do some work and get a little turquoise to help my mom." Angel gestured around the cave. "There's a lot here. Really a lot."

"No deal," Gary said. "I told you to stay away from me. This here claim is mine."

Soft wingbeats told Angel that the dragons had come down to the rancher and Celsa. Not a squeak came from his friend. She sure had guts.

"But Gary," Angel let a whine thin out his voice, "there's so much here. And I won't tell no one. It's for my mom," he repeated.

"Your mom," Gary snorted. "She's nothin' but a poor crazy woman that's going to rot in an institution. And you ain't never going to amount to anything that could help her neither."

As the unutterable rage took him, Angel raised his hands above his head, opening himself to the strength of the dragons.

"No point in begging," Gary went on, his voice rising. "I warned you. I warned you!" He cocked his gun again.

"And I warned you!" Angel roared. The dragon in him exploded into life, coursing through his blood, swelling his muscles, hardening his skin – bursting into blue scales and erupting into vast silver wings.

Gary screamed.

Angel rose from the ground, his great wings beating the cool air. Now was the time when the insults, the meanness, the hopelessness would be defeated. Now was the time the bully would pay for his soul-stabbing cruelty.

Angel roared again, letting the fire of his rage shoot into the air. Gary dropped the lantern and tried to shoot. A gibbering noise drooled from his mouth. Angel swooped toward him, beating hot air at the man's head, raking claws through his shirt.

Gary howled and tore across the floor, stumbling around columns, lurching past the cleansing pool. He fired wildly, but the bullet missed. Shrieking, he ran toward the wide passage leading to last sacred cavern.

Dizzyingly alive, Angel swooped with his razor claws extended, wild with the joy of his power, raging in hatred...

"Angel!" Celsa screamed. "Don't!"

Angel faltered, wheeling in the air as Gary plunged into the passage and disappeared. The young dragon backwinged down to the cave floor and stood listening, head cocked. Hearing footsteps, he swung his head back toward Celsa; she was walking slowly, her hand held out as if to a skittish animal.

"Don't do anything bad, Angel," she whispered. "Don't do anything that you can't get away from."

Behind her, the grandfather in human form knelt beside the rancher. The man was sitting up, but his breathing came hard and shallow; a hand clapped to the bloodstained hole in his shirt. Dragons clustered near and flew above. Their distressed keening filled the air.

"Angel!" Celsa pleaded.

Angel shook his head. *He was a dragon...*he was a boy...*he was a dragon...*

Mind whirling, he roared his frustration...and then like a butterfly settling on a cactus flower, his heart calmed. Shaking his wings, Angel felt himself ready to laugh. Instead, he snaked his head toward Celsa. She stiffened, but stared right at him, not flinching, hand still outstretched.

Angel's dragon mouth and throat were hard to form words with, but he did it. "I have a plan," he said.

Now, she jumped back, startled. "*Hay-ya-yay!* You can talk!"

"Of course I can!" A small puff of smoke swirled up from his nostrils. Liking the look of it, Angel did it again. Then he shook his mind free of its dragon-ness, while allowing his body to remain the way it was.

"*Oye,*" Celsa breathed. She extended her fingers timidly and touched the shimmering scales on his shoulder. "Hot," she said wonderingly.

Angel lifted his head and plumed a column of fire. "Hot and dangerous!" he gloated.

"Angel, don't kill Gary," Celsa pleaded. "We'll get help and he'll go to jail. Don't do anything bad, please."

"Gary will tell about this place," Angel growled. "Even Hydemann won't be able to keep people away." He stretched his wings, reveling in the vast reach and glimmer. "I have to save my people, and I have to save my mom. If my plan doesn't work out..." Angel breathed deeply. Dragon lungs were so *big*. "If it doesn't work out, take enough turquoise to buy treatments for my mom. And it won't hurt if you take some for your family, too."

"Angel!"

Ignoring her outstretched hands, he lifted into the air. The tunnel ahead was wide, almost as big as a cave itself. If Gary was waiting with his gun, Angel wanted to get in there with as much speed as he could.

"No, my son," his father begs.

"We cannot heal you in dragon form," the grandfather warns.

Angel did not answer. As the ancient songs of his people reverberated through his mind, he soared toward the enemy. This time, he would save them. He would save them all.

TWENTY-THREE

Angel backswept his wings as the passage entered the sacred cavern. It was exactly as his inherited memory remembered. The walls luminesced with the blues and greens of turquoise, sighed with cool air, and glowed with the magic of a thousand years. A ring of columns, carved with the history of his people, encircled a still pool in the center of the cave.

The pool reflected the walls and columns in eerie shades of indigo and aqua that flowed across the quiet surface to touch the bases of the columns. In the center of the pool, translucent stone reeds spiked upward, thicker and higher than reeds should grow. They surrounded a huge carving of a great, feathered serpent – Tieholtsodi. The statue glinted turquoise and gold. Between the curved talons of her forefeet, smaller rocks encircled tranquil water that lay as black as a moonless night. Angel recognized it – the watery passage to the other worlds.

Angel glided into the cavern. Old magic wove through his thoughts and being, grafting thousands of years of memory to his brief human life. This was the place of the old ones, of the grandmother, Tieholtsodi, and of the gate between worlds. Stupid Gary, to think he could savage a place like this.

But Gary still had a gun. Angel's dragon eyes caught quiet ripples from behind a column. The stench of gunpowder and Gary's meanness hung the air. Angel's anger mounted again, glistening and fire-red. It was glorious...dangerous. He sucked in a lungful of cool air – this dragon rage had to be kept under control. Celsa was right. If he gave way, he might do something that could never be fixed. And who would save his mother then?

Landing on the far side of the pool, Angel slid forward, his claws clicking loudly on wet rock – at least to dragon ears. If he could somehow grab Gary's gun...A loose stone rolled, clattering explosively into the pool.

Cra..a..a..ack...ck..ck..cr Cra..a..a..ack...ck..ck..

Angel screamed as a bullet seared his foreleg. He leapt into the air, wings thrashing, holding up his bleeding leg.

There! Twenty yards ahead, Gary stood knee deep in the pool. Shrieking pain and fury, Angel dove at his foster father.

"*No!*" Gary threw up his arms. He howled and twisted. His feet slipped from under him; the rifle splashed into the water.

Angel pounced, raising a claw wet with his own blood, ready to slash open Gary's chest. Flame darted from his drawn lips and steam hissed from his flicking tongue. Snarling, he stared down at his foster father.

Gary stared back, eyes white-ringed in terror. All the jeers, slaps and petty meanness roared in memory as Angel lifted his taloned foot higher. He would get back at Gary for everything…everything.

"*Please…no…no…*" Gary bawled.

Angel stopped…and pulled back his claws. He couldn't…he wouldn't do it.

Sobbing, Gary scuttled away, crawling, thrashing through the water on all fours. Aching and weary, Angel simply watched. He would have to let Gary go…have to let John Hydemann take him to the law.

Allowing his own blue light to illuminate the cavern, Angel gazed upward at the symbols and figures carved into the turquoise, drinking in their splendor. He didn't notice that the splashing had stopped until a flash of light glanced off the gun barrel.

Gary held the dripping rifle point blank at Angel's chest.

"You're gonna die," he snarled. "I swear I'll kill you!" He pulled the trigger. The gun clicked; it didn't fire.

Eyes locked with his foster father, Angel pulled back his magic, folded his wings and willed himself into his human form.

"Gary," Angel said. "It's me…Angel." He held out his hands and searched the man's face.

Open-mouthed, breathing hard, Gary stared back. "Angel? *Angel?*"

The gun lowered an instant, but then Gary's eyes slid past his foster son to the turquoise walls beyond. "Sorry kid, or whatever you are…" Gary raised his rifle again.

Roaring, Angel erupted back into dragon, knocking the gun from Gary's hands. The man stumbled, fell backward into the water.

Scrambling, panting, whimpering, he splashed toward the center of the pool, trying to escape.

"No!" Angel cried. Flame exploded into the air.

Shrieking, Gary splashed through thigh-deep water, slipped and fell between Tieholtsodi's claws. He shouted, gurgled, clawed the air and sank from sight.

The cave was silent; the dark pool became mirror-like again. Angel shrank back into his boy form and sagged against a column. A thin beam of a light streaked across the cave. Carrying Gary's discarded flashlight, Celsa waded through the water toward Angel. Her chin jutted out and her shoulders were back.

She gestured toward the center of the pool. "What happened to Gary?"

Angel laughed sharply. "I bet he's found more turquoise than even he could ever want. He's fallen through to the fourth world. Maybe all the way to the third world where the grandmother...where Tieholtsodi will be waiting for him." Angel sighed. "I could almost feel sorry for him."

"Well, I don't," Celsa said. "He shot *señor* Hydemann and you're bleeding, too. He deserves everything he gets. Come back to the dragons, Angel. You won't believe it. They breathed on Mr. Hydemann and he's all healed. We'll get them to breathe on you too."

Supported by his friend, Angel limped back to the cave of ceremonies. There, the rancher was standing before the grandfather, a look of dazed joy on his face. When he saw Celsa and Angel, his expression sharpened.

"Angel," he said, "are you alright?"

Angel shrugged. "Gary shot me...but it's okay, I think. He's gone."

"Gone?" the rancher demanded. "Where? You didn't...?"

"No. He fell through the passage to the other worlds. I bet we'll never see him again."

"And good riddance," Celsa turned to the grandfather. "*Por favor,*" she said. "Can you heal Angel? He's losing blood."

The old warrior smiled; the air shivered and then before them stood a silver dragon. The great being lowered his head and breathed across the boy's arm. The smell of sweet burned sugar drifted by Angel's cheeks, and warmth washed away his hurt. Strength traveled up his arm, radiating well-being and contentment.

Angel bowed his head respectfully.

"You have done well," the dragon's throaty voice whispered.

"Who are you?" Angel asked. "What are you? I saw you all dead. The boy couldn't save you."

The dragon's head lowered. "It was we who could not save him. The egg he carried – the daughter of Tieholtsodi, took her true form at sunrise. She could not heal us in death, but she drew on her mother's magic and gave us new lives as dragons. Most of our people then returned to the third world to live in that place. We have been there for a long time, but sometimes we miss the land of our old life and so we return to the sacred mountain. This man and his father and father's father's father have known our secret and keep the mountain safe for us."

Angel stared at Hydemann, shame flushing his cheeks. He had been ready to steal from him, maybe let him die. And all along the rancher had protected Angel's people and their treasures.

"What if someone found out about you?" Celsa asked the grandfather.

"If an enemy found it," he said, "we would not come back any more." He lowered his head so that silver whiskers brushed Angel's chest. "My son, will you come with us and join your family in the third world?"

Angel stared longingly at the great beast, then hunched his shoulders. "No, I can't," he said. "My mom is here. I don't belong in the third world."

"Your mother?" his father's head snaked toward him. "She is still here? Where? I have flown over these deserts for years looking for her." His breath washed over Angel. "I thought she loved me...but she went into the town for marriage clothes and never came back."

"You were going to get married?" Angel heard his voice notch up a register.

"But I lost her." The dragon's lips curled in sadness. "I would wish the chance to tell her again that she is beloved."

"She got sick," Angel said, "and then the folks made her believe mostly that she'd made you up. She's sick now, in a hospital."

His father's head reared up. Light shone along his jaw. "I will go to her, breathe on her and she will be well. And then, she can choose whether to buy her marriage clothes."

He shimmered into his human form. Angel felt a big, hysterical laugh exploding in his chest. He didn't think an Anasazi warrior could convince the doctors to discharge his mom. They'd be more likely to call the police. And would dragon magic work on the illnesses in her mind?

"No," Angel said. "I have to go to her. I'm a dragon now, and so I should be able to heal her." He glanced anxiously at the grandfather, who nodded. "I'm going to fly there, walk into the hospital as her son, and then breathe on her. If…if she gets better, I'll tell her everything and she can decide whether she wants to come back."

"My son," his father said, placing a warm hand on his shoulder, "I must go."

"And I can't let you go alone," Mr. Hydemann struck in. "Dragon or not, Angel, you're still a kid. We can take my truck."

"Your truck is in the river, and the keys to Gary's truck are probably in the third world by now," Celsa told him. "If Angel and…and his father can fly as dragons, I can ride on Angel's back and you can ride on his father. Problem solved."

"I don't need you," Angel snapped.

"Yeah, right, partner. You aren't going without me," Celsa told him. "It's a three day walk across the desert, remember? Besides, do you think I'm going to give up a chance to ride a dragon?"

"I'm not a carnival ride," Angel growled. He turned his head to hide a smile. He wouldn't mind having a friend along, especially if things didn't work out.

TWENTY-FOUR

Just as the sun was setting, they launched into the sky. Celsa sat on his shoulders just ahead of his wings and clung rather tightly to his neck. The rancher sat on Angel's father. Angel did a quick dip, just for the fun of scaring Celsa, then aimed straight for Albuquerque. Even at this distance, his dragon sight picked up the glow of city lights.

His wings beat strongly in the cool air and his keen senses caught smells and sounds he had never been aware of before. He thought about what it would be like to always feel and see like this, to be powerful and brilliant. He'd be like the myths they'd studied in school – except he would be real.

It took them nearly three hours to reach the city, and then they had to circle for awhile before Angel could find the hospital. His father's thoughts and questions drifted into his mind, like the voices in the desert, but Angel found he didn't want to answer. Instead he searched out the hospital and made his own plans.

They landed on the roof's emergency helicopter pad, their movements triggering brilliant motion sensor lights. Once on the solid surface, both Angel and his father changed to their human forms.

"You wait here," Angel told the others. "I'm going to my mom by myself."

Eyeing the warrior beside him, the rancher said. "Yes, Nah-chu-ru and I might be too noticeable."

Nah-chu-ru hesitated, and then nodded curtly. He and Hydemann eased into the shadows and sat down. Celsa however, followed Angel.

"I told you I'm going in by myself," Angel snarled at her.

"Don't be stupid," Celsa snapped back. "You'll need a lookout when you do your dragon stuff."

Angel flung through the door leading down to the hospital wards. Celsa stayed right behind him, softly closing the door.

Emerging from the stairwell on the next level, they paused and glanced cautiously up and down the corridor. To their left lay a series of offices with dim lights and closed doors. To their right, they could hear soft voices laughing from a room; at the far end an old woman tiredly swished a mop back and forth. No one else was in sight.

"Is this the psychiatric ward?" Celsa whispered.

Angel shook his head. "It's in a wing at the back of the hospital. I think we have to go down to the first floor to get to it."

Celsa pointed to an elevator across the corridor. They darted over, pushed the button and waited, trying not to look conspicuous. The old woman paused, gazed at them, and then shaking her head went back to mopping. The door opened, just as a nurse left the staff room.

"Wait," she called.

Celsa jabbed the *Door Closed* then *Lobby* button. The nurse was cut from view as the doors swooshed shut and the elevator began a slow, humming descent.

In the lobby, a man in jeans and a pajama top helped a teenager hobble in the direction indicated by the emergency department sign. Some neon-colored fish swirled back and forth in a huge tank, but there was no other sign of life. Angel loped toward the back of the hospital where the doors led to the psychiatric wing.

There was no attendant, and the doors were locked.

"Now what?" Celsa asked. "Have you got some magic power for opening locks?"

"No." Angel shook the door in frustration. His mother was back there, waiting and waiting. He could finally make her better. They could be a family – but some idiot had locked the door.

"Here." Celsa pushed a doorbell button.

"Can I help you?" A tinny voice issued from an intercom.

"Dr. Reyna, here," Celsa said firmly. "Open up, please."

The door buzzed open. Celsa grinned at Angel. "Very bad security," she whispered.

Inside, the darkened sitting room was empty. They could see movement through a half-opened door to an office.

"Be right with you," the voice, minus its tinny quality, called.

"Don't bother; we know the way," Celsa answered. She gave Angel a push. "Hurry!"

They ran across the lounge and through the first door they came to. It opened into a brightly lit hallway lined with closed wooden doors spaced about every ten feet. To Angel it looked like a nightmare – endless doors that all looked the same. How would he get to his mother before someone caught them?

"We'll never find her," he said.

Celsa shot him a scornful look and strode ahead. She stopped and tapped an aluminum frame on the wall by the door.

"The names are beside the doors," she said. "I'll take this side – you check the other."

They ran, eyes raking over nameplate after nameplate: *Rivera, Mills, White, Manza, Bettancort, Marquez, Stewart, Cerillos...*Cerillos!

"Here!" Angel stood frozen before the door. There were two names, *Cerillos* and *Hewitt*. Of course – his mother was a poor woman. She wouldn't have a room to herself.

Celsa cautiously pushed down the handle; the door swung open. The room lay half-lit by moonlight. Sockets for wires and gizmos dotted the otherwise bare walls. Identical dressers stood beside two white shrouded beds.

Ragged snores rumbled from the closest bed. Dark hair, like his mother's spilled over the pillow. Barely breathing, Angel tiptoed over and craned his neck to see the face of the woman. It was a stranger. At Celsa's inquiring glance, he shook his head. They stole to the next bed.

His mother lay on her side, eyes open, gazing out the window at the moon. Its cool light shone across her. Blinking hard, Angel leaned over and touched her thin shoulder.

"Mom," he whispered. "It's me, Angel. I've come for you." He waited. Her eyes didn't even flicker. "Mom, we're getting out of here tonight."

Nothing. Angel fought back a wave of tears, steeling himself at least to try. But what if it was no good? What if he couldn't do it?

"Now!" Celsa whispered. She pulled the curtain between the two beds, blocking the sight of the other woman.

Angel looked out at the moon, and the memory of how the desert would look in its light flooded over him. Through that memory he reached for his dragon heart. A shimmer of light and power filled the room, and from a greater height, he bent down over his mother's form.

A wave of tenderness for her – she looked so small and lost – washed over him. He breathed warm, loving air across her cheek and shoulders.

For a moment, nothing happened...and then she stirred and touched her cheek. She sighed. "I do remember that smell," she whispered. "Oh, my...it's been way too long..."

Tears seeped from her eyes and rolled down her cheeks. Still, she did not look toward the girl or dragon watching her.

Angel breathed deeply again and blew all his love and strength toward her. His mother drew in a deep breath, letting it out again in a long sigh. She blinked rapidly, then turned in the sheets, gazing up at Angel in wonder.

"Angel?" she whispered. "Is that you, baby?"

Angel nodded and let his head lower to his mother's eye level. She held out her hands and touched his cheeks. "So I ain't crazy? You are like your Daddy?"

"Yeah, I'm like my father," Angel said. "How are you feeling?"

"Good," his mother said wonderingly. "Better than for a long, long time."

"Who's there!" a voice cracked the air.

"Your roommate!" Celsa whispered.

"Lynnie! Lynnie!" Angel's mother lurched out of bed, smiled tremulously at her dragon son, and then hurried around the curtain to the other side of the room. "It's okay, hon. My son, is all. My son came to see me."

"He shouldn't be here," the woman's voice quavered. "I called the nurse. You shouldn't have visitors at night. No visitors at night. I know the rules."

"Yes, you know the rules, Lynnie," Angel's mother soothed. "But it's okay. We don't need no nurse right now."

"Too late," Celsa hissed. "Angel *change!*"

Her warning wasn't needed. Angel's dragon ears had picked up the heavy footfall in the hallway, and so he'd reached back into himself for his boy form. Celsa grabbed his arm and tugged him to the floor on the far side of the bed, just as the door opened.

A very large, very round woman, rolled into the room. A stethoscope hung around her neck. She reached over the bed and turned off the call light.

"Now Lynnie, what's happening? You have a bad dream?"

"There were people in here," Lynnie complained. "Helen had all those visitors and it's against the rules. I know the rules. I keep the rules. Everybody has to keep the rules."

"Sure enough," the nurse said. "But, there aren't any people here now, except us, so it's okay. I'll fluff up your pillow for you and you can go back to sleep, okay?"

"I suppose...but you'll watch for those kids won't you?" Lynnie asked. "I don't want no kids runnin' around here all night. I got to sleep."

"Un huh," the nurse straightened her pillow. "Now, Helen...back to bed with you, too. Everything okay?"

"Fine," Angel's mother said. "And thank you, Nurse Amaya."

The nurse eyed her thoughtfully. "My, you're feeling better tonight, aren't you, Helen?"

Angel's mother smiled. "Yes, a whole lot better. I dreamed about my son – a real nice dream."

"Did you? That's fine, then. You get back into bed and have a whole night-time of nice dreams." She waited, watching until Angel's mother climbed into her bed and pulled up the covers. His mom let her arm droop over the far side, so that her fingers caressed Angel's hair, curling the lanky strands around her fingers.

"Oh, Angel," she sighed as the nurse left and closed the door. "I been lost in here so long."

"No more, Mom," he whispered. "I'm taking you home."

Celsa helped his mother dress while Angel gazed out over the city lights. They were beautiful, but not home. Tonight he would take her home to the desert.

His mother's belongings were pitifully few – a change of clothes, his school photo, and a thin packet of cards and letters he'd sent her. She stuffed them into a plastic bag, and with the two of them holding onto her thin arms, they headed out.

"Where you goin' Helen?" the woman in the next bed sat up. "You ain't allowed to leave. And them children is back, too." Her lower lip quivered.

"I'm goin' home, Lynnie," Angel's mom said. "My boy's come for me."

Tears filled the other woman's eyes. "Then I'm gonna be alone.

I'm all alone." She shut her eyes, and clasping her knees began to rock inconsolably in her bed.

"You aren't going to be alone," Angel whispered. He drew himself into dragon form, and blew gentle healing across the woman's scrunched up face. She sighed, then breathed deeply, and without ever opening her eyes snuggled down under the covers. "I had a dog…" she murmured. "A real nice dog. My sister took him. Wonder if he still remembers me…"

"He'll remember," Angel promised softly, drawing back into his boy shape.

They walked quickly back to the elevator and went up to the roof without seeing anyone. When his mother caught sight of the warrior waiting in the shadows, she cried out and threw herself toward him. With a huge laugh, he caught her and held her tight. Then he held his hand out to his son. Angel stood for a moment, both their arms over his shoulders, happiness warming him like the rising sun streaking over the cold night desert.

"I don't want to interfere," Mr. Hydemann said after a few moments, "but if we don't leave soon, it will be morning before we clear the city."

"Yes," Nah-chu-ru agreed, his arms still holding his family protectively. He looked down at Angel. "My son, can you carry the man if I carry your mother and your friend?"

Angel nodded and shimmered back to dragon, hoping that he was in fact strong enough to carry the big rancher. They launched into the sky, just as the morning star rose over the eastern horizon.

A lot of confusing and weird things happened after that, but the hardest for Angel was to tell Treese that Gary wasn't coming back, and that he was going to live with his mom at Hydemann's ranch.

"I'm really sorry, Treese," Angel said. "But when Gary saw that Mr. Hydemann knew about him trespassing, he ran off. I doubt he'll come back, knowing that he'd end up in jail."

Treese went on drying the dishes, wiping the towel around and around her Tweetie Bird mug. "Guess that's that then," she said at last. "I've already talked to a divorce lawyer a couple of times. I just didn't know how to get away from Gary without losing my motel as well. He was like some half-starved dog and this was his only bone. Even though the motel was my parent's, he'd have fought me for it."

"Then…then you don't mind?" Angel probed.

Treese smiled and flicked the dish towel in his direction. "Mind? Yeah, I mind. But that don't change anything, and taking Gary's mean talk and attitude was bringing me down to a place I didn't want to be. I'm gonna be all right here on my own. I'm gonna make this motel into a good place again." She hung up the towel and turned toward the hallway. "Now, let's get your stuff packed up. I'm real happy for you, Angel. Your mama's a lucky woman to have a boy like you."

Angel grinned. "Thanks, Treese. And Mr. Hydemann's lucky to get a cook like my mom. She makes the best fried chicken, ever! You'll come have some, won't you?"

She ruffled his hair. "You bet, Angel. Now tell me again what Celsa's family is doing…"

Angel told her how the turquoise they'd found was going to start Celsa's family up in their own business.

He didn't say anything about his own family; only Mr. Hydemann knew that his father and grandfather had listened sadly when his mom told them that she wasn't going to buy wedding clothes after all. But just the same, she and Angel agreed that their hearts would break if they left the desert and its magic.

Every day after that, Angel got up early, went outside and climbed the highest outcropping of rock. Digging his toes into the stone for balance, he held his arms out to the sun and felt it warm the amulet against his chest. Sometimes when he saw the eagles circling above, he would leap into the air, beating his powerful wings, flying high and higher, watching for a flash of iridescent turquoise. When he caught that flicker of light, he would call out. They would come to him – his father, the grandfather, and his tribe. Together they would soar over the dry mountains, circle above the vast desert, and rejoice at being *home*.

Read the exciting companion book to

DRAGONS OF
DESERT AND DUST

DRAGONS OF
FROST AND FIRE

ONE

The floatplane touched down on Silver Lake, spewing sheets of water into the air. Pressing her icy hands against the passenger window, Kit Soriano tried to force back a shudder. This far north, the Rocky Mountains peaks thrust into the sky like teeth – old teeth, cruel teeth, with glacial lips pulled back into a snarl.

"Silver Claw," the pilot called over his shoulder. "Last stop of humanity."

David Soriano peered out his own window, then reached his hand across the seat to grip his daughter's cold fingers. Silently they stared at this terrible place where they had come to find answers. Beyond the narrow beach, a few weather-beaten buildings made up the town. Past that, mountainous ice caps blended into clouds in every direction. At the north end of the lake, a glacier hundreds of feet high lay between the mountains like a mythic sleeping monster. Aqua and blue ice shone translucent in the sunlight.

"This is what mom tried to describe…." Kit gripped the dragon-shaped knife hidden in her pocket – she was going to need every ounce of magic her mother had said it possessed. There was nothing else left for her to believe in.

The pilot eased the plane to the dock and cut the engine. Kit's ears still thrummed with the vibrations, when a series of rumbles and cracks rolled across the lake and through the skin of the plane. An ice monolith slowly split from the glacier and crashed into the water. Spray shot a hundred feet into the air. Shock waves raced across the lake, rocking the plane.

When Kit gasped and clutched the armrests, the pilot laughed. "That's Silver Snake Glacier." He pointed to the ice cliff. "In spring it breaks up some – calving, it's called. But you've never heard anything like the roars and howls that come from that ice snake in winter. I was

SUSAN BROWN   157

holed up here one year when an early blizzard rolled in. I swear I thought the noise alone would kill me."

Kit forced herself to stare impassively at the forbidding Alaskan landscape. "I'm not afraid of noise." She would not, would not let this place defeat her.

The pilot shrugged. "Hope you're not planning to stay too long," he warned. "Once winter gets her talons into this country, it can cost you your life to go outside of town."

"We'll be back in New York by winter," her father said. "We're only staying a couple of weeks."

Until we find her, Kit vowed.

The pilot heaved himself out of his chair, wrestled with the door, and showed them how to scramble down to the pontoon and then jump onto the dock. Kit shivered. Even though it was mid-August, the Alaskan air was cold through her fleece vest. She warmed up a little as they unloaded their gear.

A dozen of the town's residents drifted down to the dock, but Kit kept her eyes off the kids. Those kids had lured her mother to Silver Claw – nearly a quarter of them were albino, a genetic mutation. Dr. Nora Reits had been a genetics researcher. Nearly a year ago, she had disappeared without a trace in an early fall storm in Silver Claw.

Kit again touched the silver pocketknife nestled in her pocket. Magic find her, she prayed silently. Warmth tingled against her skin – the connection was still strong. Relieved, Kit turned her energy to separating their gear from the supplies ordered by the residents.

A lot of folks were on the dock now. In spite of herself, Kit sneaked a look under her lashes. The albino kids had snow-white hair and glacier blue eyes. Unlike some albino people, their sparkling glances showed good eyesight and they glowed with health.

"Dr. Soriano?" A big man with red hair stuck out his hand to Kit's father. "I'm Pat Kelly, mayor of this place. I wish I could welcome you here under better circumstances."

Dr. Soriano shook hands with the mayor. "We appreciate your willingness to let us get some closure on my wife's disappearance."

The mayor nodded. "I understand your feelings. We lost one of our own boys in that blizzard. This is a hard land – beautiful, but hard."

"Yes," Dr. Soriano said gazing at the ring of jagged peaks. "But I'm hoping the clinic will be a useful return for your hospitality."

"My mother-in-law will keep you busy, even if no one else does," Pat replied with an easy smile. "It's a long flight to Anchorage when the problems are the aches and pains old folks feel every time the weather changes."

As Kit reached up to grab the rest of their bags, she drew a deep breath. After all the setbacks and problems, she could hardly believe they were really here.

It had taken her father weeks to work out their journey. Getting to Silver Claw would be no problem – a regular flight from New York City to Anchorage and then they could book seats on the floatplane that delivered supplies to the town every couple of weeks. But inquiries about where to stay had been discouraging. There was apparently no reliable Internet connection that far north, and so all communication was by snail mail. A letter from the town council, signed Mary McGough, Secretary, had been brusque. The council regretted there was no hotel in Silver Claw.

Dr. Soriano's lips had thinned as he read the letter aloud to Kit.

"Isn't she the person Mom rented a room and office from? Wasn't it above a store or something?" Kit had asked.

"Yup," her dad said. "Let's try this one more time." That evening, he wrote back politely requesting that he and his daughter rent the room that his wife had previously occupied.

Three weeks later a second response from the town secretary stated that she was using the space Dr. Reits had rented for storage and so it was no longer available.

"I don't think they want us," Dr. Soriano had told his daughter over macaroni and cheese.

"I don't care. You promised me..." Kit looked challengingly into his eyes.

"And I keep my promises," he'd said. "Have some salad. It's only a little brown."

After dinner, while Kit had loaded the dishwasher and then tackled physics homework, he had written a third letter to the town council.

Dear Members of the Council,

I am hoping that we will still be able to work out the details of my daughter's and my visit. We are coming to Silver Claw. As east coast city people we don't have a lot of experience with wilderness camping, but we will come with tents and backpacks and set up on the glacier itself, if necessary.

However, I have a proposal for you. I am a medical doctor and I'm willing to operate a free clinic for the residents of the area in return for accommodation and supplies while my daughter and I are in town.

We will be arriving on August 12th, with or without a place to stay.
Sincerely,
David Soriano, M.D.

The next response came from Pat Kelly instead of the secretary and it was a lot friendlier. A new cabin had been built for his family and he was willing to let Kit and her dad use it for a couple of weeks. He sympathized with the Soriano's need to see the town where Dr. Reits had spent her last few weeks. The residents of the town would be pleased to welcome them.

Kit and her dad flew from New York on August 11th, spent the night in Anchorage and the next morning boarded the small floatplane.

After all her thinking and worrying, it seemed to Kit that she was in a dream as she stood at the edge of the dock and gazed across the wild landscape. The glacier glinted, shifting colors like a living, crystal animal.

Mayor Kelly turned from Dr. Soriano to the people standing on the dock behind him. "Here, you kids give a hand. Kirsi...Dai...grab some of the bags."

Two of the older albino teenagers, a girl and boy, left the group. Both were tall and strong, their white-blonde hair ruffling in the steady breeze. They radiated health and were incredibly good looking. Mesmerized, Kit realized with a small shock that they were better than good looking – they were the most beautiful teens she had ever seen. They were graceful, perfectly proportioned, and there wasn't even a zit to be seen. Kit thought she could hate them just for that.

As Kirsi leaned down to pick up luggage, she turned cold blue eyes toward Kit. "You shouldn't have come here," she hissed. "You soft city people don't belong." She hoisted the heavy pack over her shoulder with ease and strode away without a backward glance.

The breeze off the lake quickened. Kit shivered.

"You'll get used to the temperatures," Dai said beside her. He appeared about seventeen, a year older than she was. Up close, Kit thought his looks alone could warm her up.

Kit made a grab for her peace of mind and shrugged. "I'm not afraid of the cold."

"That's good because sometimes we get a lot of it. I'm Dai Phillips." He stuck out his hand to shake.

Kit hesitated a split second, then shook his hand. It was so very warm and firm. A responding flash of heat shot through her. This was not normal for her at all.

"I'm Kit." At home the kids either didn't touch or did hand slaps and fist bumps. Nobody under forty shook hands.

Patrick Kelly picked up one of Dr. Soriano's medical cases. "We do appreciate your willingness to run a health clinic even for two weeks, Doc," he said. "Hey there, Jancy. You, Mikey. Help the doctor with his bags." Two red-haired children each picked up a suitcase. "Dai, are you going to stand around all day or are you going to help that little girl out?"

Hot color flushed Dai's face. "Yes, Uncle Pat," he said under his breath. He reached for a duffel. "This yours, Kit?"

"I'll get it," she said. "I packed it. I can carry it." She hoisted it up and over her thin shoulder. "And I'm sixteen…not a little girl." She knew she looked too young and fragile to be in the wilderness. But she also knew that her slender bones were connected to tough muscle.

"Okay," Dai said. "But it's a bit of a hike to the cabin and I'm used to the path."

"Whatever." Kit slid the bag back to the dock, refusing to allow even a flicker of relief to cross her face. She'd jammed it with everything she thought might be useful – survival gear, guidebooks, contour maps, compass, and a Swiss Army knife.

Dai's deep blue eyes searched her own.

"What?" Kit demanded. His intense gaze unnerved her.

Dai leaned over and lifted the bag like it weighed six ounces instead of sixty pounds. "It's good you've come to us – you're the kind that's called."

"Called? Called what?"

"Called by the mountains and wilderness. By the heart that beats up there." Again, his eyes pierced her own. "Your mother was the same. You both belong here. I feel it."

Kit felt a lump rise sharply in her throat so she turned away and stared at the town as though fascinated by the worn clapboard structures. Kirsi stood at the top of the path, arms folded, looking stonily down at the people on the dock. Kit stared back defiantly.

"My mother didn't belong here and I don't either," she turned and told Dai. "I'm going to find out what happened to her and then you'll never see me again."

She picked up a bag and marched up the path toward Kirsi. Other men and children took the rest of the luggage. The remainder of the people finished unloading boxes of supplies from the plane and began hauling them up the hill toward town. Dai strode after her, whistling off-key. Kit glanced back at him. She had never seen anyone so vibrantly alive. And he had talked about her mother. Had he gotten to know her? Would he have information that would lead Kit to her?

Abruptly she slowed down, matching her steps to his. But with a cool glance, he trudged faster away from her, still whistling. Kit's eyes narrowed, but she followed without comment. In a moment she had reached Kirsi. The girl looked her over like she was a dead fish washed onto the shore.

"Stay away from Dai. He has no use for your kind," Kirsi mocked.

"What kind is that, Kirsi?" Kit demanded.

The girl's lips curled into a sneer. "A weak outlander. You'll be very sorry you ever came here." She shoved past Kit, knocking her off balance.

Regaining her footing, Kit glared after her. "I think you will be surprised." She made no effort to catch up, waiting instead for her dad and the others.

"The house is this way, Doctor." Mayor Kelly gestured along an overgrown dirt road that edged the lake. "The clinic building is in town, but this cabin has an incredible view of Silver Snake."

The cabin sat on a rounded hill overlooking the lake. The building was made of shaped logs, with a fresh look about them. Shuttered windows along the sides were wide and evenly spaced. A long porch was angled to face the glacier.

Everyone trooped through the screen door, but Kit dropped her bag and leaned on the railing, looking towards mountains and ice. Behind her, voices filled the cabin. But out here, the stillness folded into a sense of being on the edge of another world. Kit breathed deeply, tasting the tang of wilderness, and another acrid scent – sweet and bitter mingled.

She tossed her head to let the clean air wash over her. After the long despair, she was coming alive again. Kit remembered how her mother had described this place in her letters...

Silver Snake Glacier drapes the mountains like a huge sleeping animal. It really seems alive, shifting with every color that ever existed. I hope you get to see it some day – it must be one of the wonders of the world! I am going to hike up there and see if I can fathom its secrets. Something that otherworldly must have secrets, Kit. Devin tells me the glacier is riddled with crevasses and caves – a beautiful but deadly creature, I guess. It wakes when the winter storms howl over the mountains....

Dai came out on the porch and stood beside her. Despite herself, Kit was too aware of the warmth he radiated. Of those broad shoulders and lithe build. She'd never been this aware of the boys at home. Pheromones. He must be radiating mutated pheromones and she was feeling every one of them.

Another crack shattered the quiet of the town.

"Loud, isn't it?" Kit said turning to him. She froze. His eyes were a deeper blue. She'd swear they had darkened. Ridiculous. Even weird eyes, genetically mutated eyes, shouldn't change color. It had to be a trick of the light.

"This is a great time of year to be in Silver Claw." Dai's expression once again lightened to an easy smile. "There's hiking, hunting and fishing during the day and bonfires and get-togethers at night. Mary McGough at the general store gets in movies now and then."

"Sounds terrific," Kit said, "But I already have plans." She forced herself to turn away from those hot, mesmerizing eyes and look back at the cold waters of the lake. Her mother had said native legends put some kind of mythic beast in those cold depths.

Then Dai's hand, hot and strong, gripped her arm. "There are no other plans in Silver Claw," Dai told her. "You'll be smart to listen to me." The warning in his voice was unmistakable.

"Or what?" Kit challenged. How friendly or how dangerous was this guy? He was like fire and ice. Already this place was freaking her out, all beauty and danger.

His eyes shifted even darker, making that weird sense of warmth flare through her again. She didn't know whether he would have answered or not because they were interrupted by the door swinging open. The moment bled away.

"Kit," her dad called. "Which bedroom do you want?"

"Excuse me," Kit stepped past Dai and followed her father.

Inside, several men and women had settled on the sofas and chairs. Dai came in after her and crossed over to Kirsi who leaned against the far wall. As they stood talking in quiet voices and sometimes glancing in her direction, Kit felt another surge of anger. Were they talking about her? And why should she care?

In the meantime, two women were opening and shutting the cupboard doors in the kitchen area, calling on Dr. Soriano to admire how thoroughly they had stocked up for him.

"My wife is bringing some lasagna over," the mayor said. "A bit of a welcome to let you get yourself unpacked and settled tonight."

"Dr. Soriano," Dai struck in, "my mother said I'm to ask you for dinner tomorrow at seven, if you don't have other plans...." He glanced mockingly at Kit.

"Great," Dr. Soriano said. "That's very kind. We'll be there. Now Kit, what about that bedroom?"

Three bedrooms opened off the kitchen-dining-living area, so Kit chose one where the window faced the glacier. While her dad chatted with the people who had helped bring their belongings up, Kit hauled in her bags. Methodically, she unpacked her clothing and filled the drawers of the wooden dresser. She left all her survival gear in the duffel bag, zipped it up, and pushed it far under the bed.

"Kit!" her dad called. "The most marvelous dinner is being spread out here for us!"

The main room was packed with big, loud strangers. It seemed like everyone who had come down to the dock had migrated up to the cabin and brought a few friends along. Did any of those open, friendly faces hide the secret of her mother's disappearance? She wanted to shout at them, demand they tell her what they knew, but instead she forced herself to paste on a fake smile.

"Please, you must stay," her father was urging.

With only a brief show of reluctance, everyone dug into the lasagna, salad, bread and meat that all seemed to have magically appeared. Kit picked among the dishes and settled in the remotest corner of the sofa. Dai left Kirsi and perched on the arm beside her. Ignoring him, Kit took a bite of the dark meat. Flavor exploded in her senses.

"Backstrap," Dai said. "The tenderest and tastiest part of a moose."

Kit put her fork down but chewed on. It was good – different from anything else she'd tasted. "Great!" she mumbled through her full mouth.

"You're honored," Dai said. "That's probably the last of Uncle Pat's winter store. He's the best hunter in town, but we try to only hunt moose in the fall and winter."

Kit cut another piece of meat and popped it in her mouth. "The only moose I ever saw for real was in a zoo. It was big and sad looking so it seems cruel to hunt them."

"We have to eat and there aren't many fast food restaurants in the wilderness," Dai replied. "Besides, those hamburgers don't come from carrots."

Kit took a big bite of her bread to avoid answering. She knew he was right, but she didn't want to acknowledge that the rules were different here in Silver Claw. With mountains, lakes and glaciers surrounding them, they hunted to eat. They killed to survive.

A burst of laughter filled the cabin. She tried another bite of backstrap. It tasted fine on her tongue. Kit looked around at all the handsome, strong faces. She would learn what they knew, she vowed. And if they had secrets, she would find them.

Despite their protests about letting the Sorianos unpack, the townspeople didn't leave for hours. By the time Kit could finally get to bed, she was too wound up to sleep.

Outside, twilight had eased over the land, casting the mountains into dark relief. The luminous hands on her watch read 11:03 but the sky still shone dusky blue. Kit sat on her bed, wrapped in a quilt, looking out toward Silver Snake Glacier.

It drew her, called her, just as Dai had said it would. Her mom's letters had described the hours she spent hiking by the glacier. She'd written that the sight and sound of the ancient ice relieved her frustrations when the townspeople refused to cooperate with her research.

And that's how I'll start, Kit decided; she would go to the places her mother had described, try to find some kind of clue her mother may have left behind. Looking out the open window at the immense distances and peaks, Kit wondered with a sinking heart whether she would be able to find the places from the descriptions in the letters. In New York, hemmed in by buildings and streetlights, she had not been able to grasp the vastness of the landscape.

Her father came in, set a lantern on the table beside her bed and sat down.

"They seem like nice people around here," he said at last.

Kit rolled her eyes. "That's what Mom said...until they found out what she was doing."

Her hand slipped under her pillow to touch the knife and the packet of letters. In the last one, Nora Reits had written in an excited scrawl from her office over the general store. She had said she would try to slip the letter into the outgoing mail sack before the floatplane arrived. This flight, she was sure, would bring lab results for the blood samples she had coaxed from one albino boy. Kit got the letter two days after her mother disappeared.

"Kit, it was a simple hiking accident," her dad said. "You know she hiked up there alone, even though the weather was threatening."

"Then why did the lab results disappear?" Kit demanded. "And the searchers didn't find a body. They're keeping her somewhere. I know it! My knife...."

"Kit, don't start about that knife again." Her father rubbed his hand over his face; his eyes were exhausted. Kit fell silent.

If only he would believe what Kit knew against all reason was true. Her mother was alive.

Another crack reverberated through the air. The lantern flickered. Somewhere, out there, Kit knew her mother was alive.

TWO

Her father went to bed. Kit heard him moving around, then a sharp creak of bedsprings and a sigh as he settled in. A few moments later, soft snores drifted through the cabin.

Wide awake, Kit stared out at the far northern twilight remembering the last conversation she had had with her mom.

Their Upper West Side apartment had been warm for New York in late May, but Kit had woken up with the blankets wound around her shoulders as though shielding herself from icy winds. The nightmare of ice and muffled screams had left her shaking. Her mom had heard, and as always, had come to comfort her. Except for the faint bloom of streetlights, the room was dark.

"Mom, don't go to Silver Claw," Kit pleaded. She knew she sounded childish, but with the nightmare still throbbing through her, she didn't care. "I have a terrible feeling about it."

Dr. Reits unpeeled her daughter from the mound of blankets and held her hands tightly. "Kit, I have to go. I'm a scientist and I received a research grant because an adventurer up there claimed a quarter of the kids in Silver Claw show signs of genetic mutation." She grimaced. "That sounds like a bad science fiction movie, doesn't it? No wonder you're spooked. But it won't be like that, really – and you're too old to need me around all the time."

"It isn't that," Kit insisted. "It feels...cold."

"That far north, it'll be cold all right. Snow caps, glaciers and mountain peaks." She startled as the roar of a motorcycle reverberated like a gunshot from the street below.

"Don't go, mom," Kit repeated. "Or let's all go. You and me and dad. He'd like to do research on this too."

"I know. First time he's been jealous of me. But you know he's committed to that lecture series. And you have the state track meet. You have a great shot at winning."

"I don't care. We can cancel."

"Nope. We keep our promises in this family," her mom said. "Besides, it's an honor your dad was offered those lectures and another that I was awarded this grant. And your team is counting on you."

"What about our family?" Kit demanded. "Stay mom...please."

"Kit, we stick together and take care of our own. But that doesn't mean we don't change or grow. Time apart won't matter if we love each other." She hesitated, then took a thin chain from around her neck and held it up. From the end hung a slim folded knife worked in the shape of a dragon. A small red gem, the dragon's heart, shone in the weak light. "I wasn't going give this to you yet, Kit, but maybe you need it. It's very special. It's supposed to be magic."

"I'm not a baby, mom." Kit hunched the blankets back up over her shoulders. I only feel like one, she thought bitterly.

The knife twisted slowly, suspended in air. The silvery reflection seemed to grow, to throw more and more light around the room.

"This came from my great-grandmother, Joanna MacLachlan," her mom said. "She headed north to make her fortune in the Klondike Gold Rush in 1899. When she came out of the bush into Skagway two years later, she brought a baby – your grandmother – and this knife. She would never say what happened, who she had been with or who gave her the knife. But she did say it was northern magic – a native shaman's artifact for connecting two worlds. The dragon will keep the fire of life in your heart and the silver will find the souls of the people you love."

"Yeah, right." Kit muttered. "And the native mythology is full of dragons."

Her mother half-smiled. "You'd be amazed what the legends say – that there are worlds apart in the sky, earth and sea. But the right artifact and a gifted shaman can connect them all."

Her mom continued to hold the knife in the half-light, letting the silver shimmer like a beacon.

Kit resisted the urge to reach for it. "How does it work?" she asked finally.

"I don't know," her mom said. "But my grandmother claimed that as long as the dragon's heart is warm, you'll know the people you care about are alive."

With a quick flick of her wrist she caught up the knife, letting the chain loop and dangle through her fingers. Opening Kit's hand, she pressed the knife and chain into it.

"Here, Kit. It's yours now. Until you pass it on to your own daughter. Keep it near you. When you touch the dragon's heart, the heat will tell you I'm still safe up there in the frozen north."

Kit opened her hand slowly. The knife lay across her palm, about six inches long, with the blade folded in – larger, stronger than a standard pocketknife. The silver handle was embossed with intricate symbols and whorls that coalesced into the form of a dragon. Beautiful. Delicate. Deadly.

"It looks old," Kit said. "Older than your great-grandma would have been." She turned it over, watching the light play across the design, and then touched the heart etched in the dragon's chest. Warmth spread from the handle to her hand. Hotter than her own skin temperature.

"Is it working?" her mom asked.

Kit nodded. "Why? How?"

Her mom touched the knife with her fingertip. "I'm a scientist, Kit. I've thought of every scientific theory I know and every time I come up blank. It shouldn't work – but it does. Grandma said it was a shaman's magic for finding lost souls. There were so many things she knew that people don't bother with any more. She said this magic came from the silver and that the silver had been given by someone who had loved her more than the world itself." She paused watching the hypnotic spin of light. "So long as the dragon's heart is warm, you'll know I'm fine. I can't explain, but I promise it's true."

She kissed Kit on the forehead. "Slide it under your pillow," she advised, "and check it each night. Then you'll know everything's okay...and that Dr. Nora Reits, geneticist extraordinaire, is making the discoveries of a lifetime. You know how much I want this, Kit."

Kit nodded, slipped the knife under the pillow and slid down under her blankets. "Well, if you take too long, I'll come find you. That's a promise."

"I'll be counting on it." She tucked the blankets around her daughter. "Two months – three at the most. With all the things you have planned this summer, you'll hardly know I'm gone..."

Except her mom hadn't come back.

Three weeks after school began, Kit's world disintegrated. First her dad had been in a head-on that left him cut, bruised and unable to walk.

Then there had been the night of the phone calls. Alaskan state troopers reported Nora Reits had been lost in an early blizzard. It seemed to Kit she did not sleep for days after that, though she supposed she must have. Her friends looked at her in stricken silence and clumsily tried to comfort her. And then as the weeks spun past Halloween, everyone gave up hope. On the December night of the memorial service for her mom, she had her first dream.

She stands on a mountain overlooking a town. The sun fades and she is wrapped in cold night, dark as a tomb.

"Mom!" she shouts. "Mom!"

An old lady dressed in the clothes of a century before trudges up the mountain path. Kit doesn't even wonder why she can see when the night is so black. Closer and closer the old woman comes.

"Well, d'you have a light?" she asks crossly.

Kit reaches into her pocket and holds out the knife. Light glows from the handle, stronger and stronger, until it gleams like a star. The dragon etched in the silver begins to move, beating its wings, bursting into life before Kit.

"Ah, Devin, my love," the old lady croons. But she isn't old, any longer. She is young and laughing as she climbs on the dragon's back and flies away into the night.

Kit stands alone on the mountaintop, holding the knife. Her grief freezes her blood and mind, beyond tears. She looks down at the knife in her hand...

Three nights in a row, Kit awoke from the same dream of the old woman on the mountain before she remembered the knife. Magic. Magic that might find her mother. Frightened, desperate, Kit searched through her drawers until her hand touched cold metal. Where the streetlight below cast a beam of light through her bedroom window, Kit held up the knife, watching it twist this way and that on its silver chain. Light flickered off the etching, giving the illusion that the dragon wings were beating. Remembering what her mother had said, Kit at last touched the heart of the dragon.

Instantly, heat glowed through her fingertip.

"Mom," she whispered, willing it to find her mother. But then the air around the sides of the knife misted with cold. And the knife itself, all but the dragon's heart, frosted with crystals of ice.

"No!" Kit cried and dropped it. In the time between when the knife left her hand, and the handle touched the floor, the ice disappeared. The knife bounced under her bed.

"Kit! What is it?" Her father, disheveled from sleep leaned on the door. "Nightmares again?"

Blinking tears, she had nodded. He had hugged her, offered her hot chocolate and then tucked her in as he had done when she was a child. Then, with the meager comfort of that gone, he had sat beside her, head in hands while tears silently ran down his cheeks. Leaning against his shoulder, she had said nothing then about the knife. But the next day, in full afternoon sun, she had hunted under the bed, held up the knife, and again touched the heart of the dragon. Once again, a jolt of warmth shot through her hand, while hoar frost spiked the knife's silver edges.

Heat and ice.

So long as the dragon's heart is warm, you'll know I'm fine.

But the ice? What did it mean?

The dragon's heart is warm...

The ice...

She'd made a promise...

She would go find her mother...

It took Kit months of planning and pleading. The nightmares solved it. Desperate her father took her to a psychologist, and surprisingly, she sided with Kit.

"Your daughter believes her mother is still alive because she's had no closure," Dr. Fiske had said to Kit's father. She leaned forward. "Going to the place where her mother disappeared may help." Kit sat up straight, willing her father to agree.

Dr. Soriano sighed deeply, like the air going out of a balloon. "Last week my sister said I should start dating again and I felt like she'd suggested I cheat on my wife. Maybe going to Silver Claw for a couple of weeks will help us both. When Nora disappeared…when we got that phone call…it was two days after I'd been in the car accident. I couldn't even go help the searchers…"

"Dad," Kit took his hand, "I know mom's alive and I have to look for her."

"Kit, it's impossible. It's been almost a year!" Their eyes locked over the old argument.

"I promised," Kit had said. "I know it sounds crazy, Dad. But I promised."

Her father's exhausted eyes had filled up, too much to speak. But he had nodded yes.

That had been in May, but because of the letters from Mary McGough, it had taken Dr. Soriano weeks to finalize their travel plans.

In a fret of impatience, Kit packed, repacked and again and again checked her research. She had stopped answering her friends' calls and texts, and the parties that had seemed so important a year before were forgotten. All winter long, when she told her father she was doing homework, she had been searching for information about the town and area – or trying to. She had entered keyword after keyword – nothing. The internet carried more tidbits of facts than the world could use, but all Kit could find out was that Silver Claw had begun as a mining town over a hundred and twenty years before. Unexplained accidents and bitter weather had wrecked the venture. Local tribes claimed that legendary monsters were responsible and avoided the area. Other than the original settlers, only a few people stayed after the mine closed.

Now, all these years later, the town would have been forgotten, Kit guessed, if that adventuring journalist hadn't mentioned the genetic albinoism in a travel article. Kit's mom had seen the article, connected native legends, applied for and then gotten a grant to research the phenomenon.

Three months after they put her on the plane to Alaska, Kit and her dad got the call from the state troopers that Dr. Nora Reits had disappeared in an early fall blizzard. Townspeople searched by snowmobile and snowshoe. State troopers searched by air. There was no trace of the woman or the teenager who was with her. And when Dr. Reits' personal belongings were sent home, her research notes had vanished.

Each night and each morning, Kit's fingers searched out the silver knife on its thin chain. Each time it was the same. The rim hoared with frost, but the red gem still glowed warm to her touch. The center was her mother's heart – and it was warm.

Kit had known, known that her mother was not dead.

THREE

Drifting through vast empty chambers that shimmer with hues of aqua and blue, Kit stretches and swirls into cracks and crevices. Great white shapes half-open blue eyes and gaze at her in mild curiosity, as if she is part of their dreams. She flows on, silent and without purpose until she is in a small ice cave. She sees her mother, encased in a column of ice, her frozen hands pressing against the sides. A great shape, all claws and dull scales, curls around the column, sleeping.

"Mom!" Kit cries.

"Mom!"

The sound of her own voice woke Kit. Gasping, she pressed the knife close, willing warmth to stream from her own heart to her mother's in that cold, cold place.

She forced her shaking legs to thrust out of the blankets and walk out onto the porch. Leaning against the railing, she stared upward at the mountains and Silver Snake Glacier. As the clean air rippled into her body, her shuddering muscles relaxed.

Above, the skies flashed with wheeling birds, their trills, whistles and squawks filling her ears. Distant valleys and ravines showed as deep purple slashes against the mountains. Trees carpeted the lower slopes in inky emerald. Farther up, the color changed to luminous green where moss and grass took over. Finally toward the summits, the mountains darkened to bare rock, capped with year-long snow. Kit spotted half a dozen white dots moving against the steep slope – mountain goats or sheep. High above, a bald eagle screamed and dodged a black and white magpie. Kit's eyes were pulled back to the lake by a flicker and splash – fish jumping in the early light.

Beautiful. Beyond beautiful. But even as her heart lifted with the splendor and peace of it, her knuckles whitened on the railing. Her mother had disappeared in this place. Kit touched her knife. The edges were still cold but the center warmed hotter than ever before.

I'm coming, Mom, she promised. I'm coming for you soon.

An hour later Dai arrived. Whistling shrilly, he hammered on the door. Reading over breakfast, Kit and her dad looked up from their books and grinned at each other.

"Not exactly like New York," her dad murmured.

"Are you up, Kit?" Dai called through the screen into the shadows.

Kit downed a last gulp of milky coffee and opened the door.

"Morning," Dai said. The sun glinted off his hair. He was dressed as yesterday in a tee shirt, faded jeans, and scuffed hiking boots. A backpack hung over one shoulder. "Hi, Dr. Soriano! Mrs. Stone wants to know when you'll have your clinic open. Her knees are swollen up bad again, so she wants you to look at them. And Uncle Pat said to tell you the office is set up. You just have to hang out your shingle."

Dr. Soriano spread another glob of homemade blueberry jam on his toast. "Thanks, Dai. I can take a look at her knees this afternoon. But if there's any real problem, she'll have to fly out to Anchorage to the hospital there."

"Oh, she knows that," Dai replied. "Kit, Uncle Pat asked me to show you around. We don't want you getting lost on your first day, do we?" His voice only mocked slightly.

She smiled brightly. "Don't do me any favors. I'm just fine on my own."

"No you aren't," he replied. "The wilderness is no place for soft, city girls."

Kit's temper flared. "Sure of yourself, aren't you?"

"Yes ma'am." His eyes shimmered with amusement. "If we were in New York, I would follow your advice. I'd be the soft one then."

Uncertainly Kit eyed him. "I don't think soft is the word I'd use. Stupid maybe."

His mouth widened to a grin. An irresistible grin, Kit thought resentfully. Of course he deserved to be snubbed, completely crushed in fact. But then, she might need him. And he was very easy on the eyes. Regardless, there was no way she was going to meekly fall in line at his orders. She dropped her eyes for an instant, then resolutely lifted her chin. "Sorry. I told you I have plans."

Dai glanced at Dr. Soriano. Her father cleared his throat. "Kit, why don't you spend the day with Dai?" he asked. "You'll have more fun being with someone who knows the area."

"I'm not here for fun," Kit replied flatly.

"We know this is a dangerous place," her father said. "You aren't so foolish as to wander around these mountains like it was some kind of theme park. Dai is an experienced outdoorsman."

"Dr. Soriano," Dai interrupted, "if she doesn't want me, that's okay. I have other things to do."

"I don't want you!" Kit snapped. Frustration, hurt and anger struggled for supremacy in her. Didn't her father get it? Dai would be spying on her for the town, for the people that she was sure had conspired to cause her mother's disappearance.

"Kit," her dad said sharply, "this is a kind gesture. The mayor explained that the residents didn't want us to come because your mother..." he took a breath and went on. "...your mother's inexperience with the way of life here caused her to take such...risks." His face was pale. "We...I can't expose you to the same dangers."

"Dad! I know the risks!" Kit cried. "And mom had that other boy, Devin with her!"

"Dev should've known better." Dai's voice smoldered, and now his eyes were nearly navy. "He wasn't a great woodsman, but he should've known the weather was turning. He should've felt it in his blood."

"The point is," Kit's father said, "either you accept Dai as a guide or you spend your time helping me in the clinic."

"Fine!" Kit snapped. She turned to Dai. "I'd like to see the library, please. My mother wrote me that it's the oldest building in the town. If visiting a library isn't too dangerous around here!"

"Kit," her father said warningly.

Dai said nothing but his eyes went smoky at her rudeness. In spite of herself, Kit felt a flush creep over her cheeks. This guy was getting under her skin and she didn't like it. Not even a little bit.

She refused to look at either of them as she slung her own backpack over her shoulder and strode out the door ahead of Dai. A tour of historic Silver Claw had not been part of her plan and she chafed with frustration. Before breakfast, she had packed her bag with a guidebook, folded survey map of the region, beef jerky, a full water bottle and compass. In the pocket she'd stashed waterproof matches, a Swiss army knife, four energy bars and a feather-light Mylar survival blanket. All her reading about the wilderness had taught one important lesson – be ready for disaster.

But none of the books had prepared her to be so thoroughly thwarted by her father.

Lips clamped shut, Kit ran down the steps. She would have liked to outpace Dai, but his long legs and easy stride made that impossible. She was aware of his steady glances as they walked.

After several minutes of stalking, seething silence, he touched her arm.

She stopped and glared up at him. "What?"

"It's going to be a bad two weeks for you like this," Dai remarked.

"Can't you get it through your head that I'm not here to have fun," Kit ground out. "In case you forgot, this is where I lost my mother. I need to do some things..." She looked down at the path, fighting for control.

"So, what are you needing to do, Kit – for your mother?" Dai spoke slowly, searching her face as if trying to look right inside her.

Kit sucked in her breath, hard. Not even Dr. Fiske had asked her what she needed to do. People talked over and around her as if all she needed was the right comfort blanket to get her to forget her mother's disappearance. They didn't understand that she needed to do something – not just wait to get over it.

Could Dai help her?

No, she told herself. It's too dangerous. You don't know why he is really here.

"I want to go to the places my mother went to," Kit lied, barely able to keep her voice from quivering. "Mom wrote me letters that described her hikes and what she saw in detail – a lot of detail. I want to see everything she saw. It will help give me closure." At least that's what Dr. Fiske said, she thought bitterly.

She glanced at Dai under her lashes, looking for some kind of a reaction. His eyebrows drew together and he continued to gaze intently at her, but said nothing. Kit wondered suddenly if the mayor had told him to keep her away from anything – to guard the town's secrets. She would not trust him.

"So," Kit said briskly, "are you going to show me all the sights of

Silver Claw?"

"The library's at the end of the main street," Dai said.

"There's more than one street?" Kit asked, pretending to be incredulous.

Dai's thoughtful expression lightened. He gestured toward the town. "This is a thriving metropolis – we have three streets."

In spite of herself, Kit laughed and was rewarded by an answering grin. Why was he so good looking? Why did the sight of his easy movements make her skin tingle with warmth? It made it so hard to remember he might be the worst person she had ever met, and she had to remember that. He might even be in on the secret of her mother's loss. Pushing the confusion of her thoughts aside, she turned toward town, matching his long, fast strides.

"After the library, we can keep looking around, or go get a soda and burger at Mary's store – whatever you want," Dai said. "If you want to head out of town, we can hike up along the lake path to Dead Man's Falls." He hesitated. "I know Devin showed that to your mom, and she liked to picnic there."

Kit nodded. "That would be good."

A few minutes later, they reached the dock where the main street ran upward to the town. Kit saw that the buildings, if they had ever been painted, had lost their colors and faded to the same muted greys and browns as the boulders and snags dotting the slopes. The landscape Kit and Dai had passed was brightly splashed with alpine wildflowers. In the town's window boxes and gardens, riots of color competed for the eye.

"Wow!" Kit exclaimed. "I thought the winters killed everything. How can they grow all this?"

Dai followed her eyes. "People spend a lot of time gardening," he said. "It makes up for the long winter when everything's white."

Kit stopped by a fence where scarlet roses grew as high as her head. Beside them, bright yellow day lilies tufted out of black dirt. Kit leaned over and sniffed.

Sweet flower scents wafted through the air. Under them came another smell, earthy, like old ashes. Thoughtfully Kit brushed her fingers over the delicate petals of a flower she didn't recognize. She remembered a paragraph in one of her mother's letters:

You should see the flowers around here. They are bigger and brighter than anything I've ever seen. I'm sure some of them are tropical, so I don't know how they get them to grow. Either they use magic or there's more genetic mutation going on here than I suspected. I'll need plant and soil samples too. The key to this mysterious genetic mutation might be embedded in the natural environment....

"What am I smelling?" Kit sniffed the sweet and smoky smell. "What do they use for fertilizer?"

"Manure and regular fertilizers, I guess," Dai said. "I don't know much about gardening. You should ask Violet Furrow or my mom."

Kit sniffed again. She strained to identify the smell...she should recognize it. Squeezing her eyes shut, she let the scent carry her... drifting upward on the breeze, breathing gulps of the sweet smokiness as great white wings beat in the sunlight...

Kit shook her head, to clear the vision. Was being here in this town causing her to dream while awake? The night terrors were enough; if she had to endure them during the daytime, she didn't know how she could stand it.

There had to be something in the fertilizer. Maybe a narcotic or...or some weird chemical. Or maybe the plants had been genetically altered like her mom suspected, creating a drug right in their scent. What was happening in this town that changed the living things?

Dai walked on ahead, but she lingered and sniffed again. A surge of heat flashed in the knife under her sweater. She pulled up the chain and gripped the knife. Hot. The center was hotter than ever.

What was going on? How could that smell burn a stronger link to her mother? What was feeding the magic in her knife?

Want to read more? Dragons of Frost and Fire at Amazon.com: http://tinyurl.com/DragonsofFrostandFire

About the Author…

Adventure, mystery, and magic propel Susan Brown, fueling her imagination into writing more and more stories for her favorite audience of teens.

Susan skillfully combines two careers that she loves – teaching intermediate and high school students, and of course…writing! Perhaps some of her students will hear the echoes of their passionate voices in the stories she writes.

Susan lives with her two border collie rescue dogs amid wild woods and overgrown gardens in Snohomish County, Washington. From there she supervises her three daughters, assorted sons-in-law and two grandsons. It's a great way to be a writer!

Find more information, free stories, and news about upcoming books at: www.susanbrownwrites.com

Susan is also one half of Stephanie Browning, the pen name shared with her writing partner of close to a thousand years, Anne Stephenson – www.stephaniebrowningromance.com

Made in the USA
Coppell, TX
30 January 2021

49102752R00105